The Souls of Clayhatchee
A Southern Tale

By Anthony Todd Carlisle

Hidden Shelf Publishing House
P.O. Box 4168, McCall, ID 83638
www.hiddenshelfpublishinghouse.com

THE SOULS OF CLAYHATCHEE

Copyright © 2021, Anthony Todd Carlisle
Hidden Shelf Publishing House
All rights reserved

Artist: Megan Whitfield

Graphic design: Kristen Carrico

Interior layout: Kerstin Stokes

Editor: Megan Whitfield, Robert D. Gaines

Publisher's Cataloguing-in-Publication Data

Names: Carlisle, Anthony Todd, author.
Title: The Souls of Clayhatchee : A Southern tale / by Anthony Todd Carlisle.
Description: McCall, ID: Hidden Shelf Publishing House, 2020.
Identifiers: LCCN: 2020912538 | ISBN: 978-1-7338193-9-8 (Hardcover) | 978-1-7338193-8-1 (pbk.) | 978-1-7354145-0-8 (ebook)
Subjects: LCSH Clayhatchee (Ala.)--Fiction. | Alabama--Fiction. | Family--Fiction. | Murder--Fiction. | African Americans--Fiction. | Southern states--Fiction. | Racism--Fiction. | Mystery fiction. | BISAC FICTION / African American / Mystery & Detective | FICTION / African American / General
Classification: LCC PS3603. A752585 S68 2020 | DDC 813.6--dc23

Printed in the United States of America

Table of Contents

Chapter 1 – The Trip Home 5
Chapter 2 – Dirty South 19
Chapter 3 – The Benefactor 34
Chapter 4 – Shadows 40
Chapter 5 – The Woman in Black 44
Chapter 6 – An Unspeakable Horror 50
Chapter 7 – Stomping in my Timbs 62
Chapter 8 – Do a Little Dirt 65
Chapter 9 – Brother Man Down 74
Chapter 10 – Stay Strong 76
Chapter 11 – Pudding 82
Chapter 12 – The Ghost Killer 86
Chapter 13 – Stirring up the Spirits 95
Chapter 14 – Meeting M 101
Chapter 15 – Killing Daddy 105
Chapter 16 – Been Dead 113
Chapter 17 – Bunky's Revelation 117
Chapter 18 – They Here 122
Chapter 19 – The Family Gathering 125
Chapter 20 – No Po Po 136
Chapter 21 – The Big Payback 143
Chapter 22 – Ghosts in the Closet 150
Chapter 23 – Handle That 155
Chapter 24 – Two White Crackers 158
Chapter 25 – Secret Places 160
Chapter 26 – Unearthing 168
Chapter 27 – Dear Mama 171

Author's Note
The South of My Childhood

My grandparents were part of the great twentieth-century migration of African-Africans who left their homes in the South to find a better life in the North. Settling in early 1950s Pennsylvania, Perry and Ellen Carlisle found a community of other like-minded expatriates looking for societal and economic freedoms. It was never easy, but they settled into domestic life with my grandfather clocking decades at Aliquippa's J&L Steel and my grandmother raising six children and later a grandchild, me, in their Ambridge community just outside of Pittsburgh.

Even so, Perry and Ellen never strayed far from their southern roots in speech, cuisine, attitude, and pride. It was within that pride they connected their children to the family's ancestral home of Troy, Alabama. The summer trips spent in Troy with my relatives provide me with some of my greatest childhood memories.

About forty-five miles down the road from Troy was the town of Clayhatchee. I always loved that name, a place that just sounded like the South. While the Clayhatchee of this story is fictional, to me it represents the many small towns in the South whose histories are both colorful and tainted.

For the experience of Troy and so much more, I dedicate this book to the memory of Perry and Ellen Carlisle. Your legacies whisper your names in love and seek out your eternal wisdom, guidance, and strength.

Chapter 1
The Trip Home

I was heading back home. Not the home I knew as a child, but a home that was mine all the same. It was the beloved home of my mother in all of its Jim Crow past. It was the home of my father, who barely survived it with all of his ornery ways. It was the home of their parents and their parents' parents, who picked cotton, sharecropped, and worked the land until they no longer could. And it was home to their ancestral enslaved parents who toiled day and night under the firm grip of massa's whip. Clayhatchee, Alabama was my inherited home—collard greens, black-eyed peas, chitterlings, string beans, sweet yams, cornbread, and all. It was a home that I needed to get back to... more than I could ever know.

Mama was dead and Daddy had died six months earlier. But it was Mama who made me leave New York—my job, my plush condo, my ex-girlfriend—and drive 1,130.38 miles and nearly nineteen hours on I-81 South. Mama made it back home before I did. Well, Mama's body made it there, where it was received by her sister, Aunt Dee. Mama desperately needed to be buried in Clayhatchee, even after building a life in the North for more than half a century.

Mama told Daddy she would go back home someday, but Daddy had been adamant about never returning. That place meant nothing to him but rednecks, crackers, abuse, and oppression. He was too old now for any of that foolishness and thought it was a damn fool notion for Mama to return. Mama argued that things had changed, that the South they knew no longer existed. She would tell Daddy how the South had elected Black mayors, council members, sheriffs, and judges; and that Black people had really moved up the ladder to become middle class. All that "foolishness" they knew was over. Daddy, though, never bought it. And for Mama's part, she kept threatening the old man that she would leave him and make her way home.

If she really wanted to leave Daddy, Mama had her pick of reasons, starting with his cheating ways. Daddy loved women and women loved Daddy. Mama, for years, looked the other way until one day she stopped and looked Daddy square in the eyes. He had to make a choice between having a lifetime of true love with his wife and kids or having fleeting moments from an array of low, no-account fast women. Daddy chose correctly and remained in good marital standing for the rest of his life. Nonetheless, he remained hard as steel. Hard on Mama, hard on his children, hard on life. Daddy carried around a mean streak that kept him from fearing any man and one that called on those he encountered to respect him always or to disrespect him at their own peril. One thing for certain, Daddy loved Mama, and he would kill for her. And Mama loved Daddy, even with all his disagreeable ways.

Soon after Daddy died, Mama was planning a trip to Clayhatchee, announcing that she would be returning with a surprise. She was excited about returning home. Clayhatchee had grown from the small, clay dirt town of the 1930s and '40s that she and Daddy knew when they were young. Now, in 2004, it was a small city featuring quaint neighborhoods and historic districts. The community of 18,000 residents promoted itself as a tourist destination, particularly to those interested in the mid-twentieth century civil rights struggle. It was the home of Clayhatchee University, which transformed from a small state teachers' college in the nineteenth century to a world-class education center of research and technology.

Mama was making preparations to visit her childhood home when she suffered a stroke. With each passing day, deterioration made her less my mama—the woman who had remained vibrant and energetic as she aged—and more of an unrecognizable, feeble old woman who seemed to welcome death. Just four months after suffering her stroke, Mama had become bedridden, going in and out of consciousness. The doctor said she was dying. With that, the family rallied around Mama to ensure her affairs were in order. It was during this time that Mama, in a moment of clarity and consciousness, made me promise that her final resting place would not be Pittsburgh, but the dark rich soil of Clayhatchee.

As I took exit 79, I felt a gush of heat so intense it seemed to singe my eyebrows. The air was thick, making my breathing a concerted effort between my brain and lungs. It was the type of heat that gives the illusion the air is on fire.

As much as the South claimed its modernity, I felt as if I had been transported to an early period. The homes located just off the exit were more shanty than houses and the spacing of the homes provided a sense of desertion. At one shanty home, a dark-skinned boy—couldn't be any older than four—stood on the wooden porch, barefoot and shirtless. Behind him, a young girl opened the screen door, a smaller child on her hip.

In all that emptiness, a BP gas station seemed to sprout. I needed a drink, gas, and, as always, directions. It wasn't that I was lost. I just didn't want to become lost.

"How close am I to Clayhatchee?" I asked the white clerk. She was round, puffy, and middle-aged, with black-rimmed glasses that intersected with her brown curly hair. She had a generous smile.

"Honey, you're about a half an hour away. Just stay on this street until you see Route 8 and then make a left. I live in Clayhatchee. Where exactly are you trying to go?"

"I'm trying to find 146 Robinson Road."

"Oh, I can tell you how to get to Robinson Road. Route 8, after two miles, turns into Robinson Road. You will see MLK Elementary School on your left. Go past MLK, but don't go past Mount Zion Baptist Church or you've gone too far. It's a straight shot, pretty simple. You have a good day, sweetie, and welcome to Clayhatchee."

Not the reception I thought I would receive from the first white person I encountered in the land of Dixie. I had seen those PBS specials—Black folks marching, attack dogs barking, white people shouting, and redneck police officers swinging clubs. It couldn't be the South my father fled in 1949, but I had been mentally preparing myself for whatever residual racist attitudes lingered from the sting of nearly three hundred years of slavery and another hundred years of

Jim Crow torture, degradation, and discrimination. I didn't care what Mama said, racial problems persisted in the North, so I was certain they hadn't been eradicated in the South. It didn't matter how many schools we integrated, lunch counters we ate at, how many millions we made singing, dancing, running, shooting, and catching, or how many white girls or boys we were humping, racism was alive and well and breathing lustily throughout America, North and South.

No, heading this far down South had never appealed to me. Plus, I'm its worst nightmare—an educated Black man who didn't ascribe to King's position of turning the other cheek. *If you don't know, now you know... baaaby, baaaby.*

But I admit to being curious about my parents' heritage and how much had changed in the land of cotton. I wanted to see what it was about, maybe uncover some buried family secrets and fossils. Something significant had occurred there. Mama would not let it go and Daddy chose not to remember. I wanted to know what it was.

Why did my mother love this place? Why did my father despise it? How much different would my experience be from hers, from his, from theirs? Why did she have to be buried here and, more importantly, why did I have to be the one to do it?

When I left for Alabama, it was just to bury Mama. Turns out I was going there for much more than I could have ever imagined. The rattling from ghosts of the past grew louder the closer I came to Clayhatchee.

> *"You're a dead nigger," Petey Smalls said, just before his throat was slashed.*
>
> *Smalls fell to the ground, clutching his neck and gasping for air. The powerfully built Black man stood over Petey, now flailing on the ground. After wiping the blood off his shiny blade with a white handkerchief, he tucked the weapon into his pocket.*
>
> *"That makes two dead crackers tonight. Just one more to go," the Black man said, before disappearing into the night.*

****

CARLISLE

During my drive to the South, I had thought about how nothing had been simple about this trip. I was rushing to meet with relatives whom I hadn't laid eyes on since I was fourteen. I was planning my mother's second funeral and it had to be quick, no more than three days. I loved Mama, but I needed to get back to my life and my job as a reporter at the *New York Daily News*. I needed to finish the last piece of my four-part series about corruption in City Hall that had consumed nearly a year of my life. It had everything—sex, drugs, money, and race. My editor, Ed Cuddy, had pushed to get the series finished. I was almost there. I needed to nail down these final interviews, write quickly, and ship my story off to my slave-driving editor. Cuddy, in a human moment, told me that I didn't need to finish the piece this week; that he had waited for it this long (from the world's slowest reporter) and just to take care of my family's business. But I was becoming anxious. The story couldn't hold much longer, and I didn't want to be scooped. I needed to take care of Mama's business so I could take care of my own.

We had already said our goodbyes to Mama with a large ceremony in Pittsburgh. All of Mama's friends and church members were there, as was our Northern family. Reverend Walker officiated, reminding us how Elaine had been a faithful servant to the Lord. She served First Baptist Church in Homewood for nearly half a century—in the senior choir, as a deaconess, and later as a church elder mother. Reverend Walker said Sister Elaine was now standing before the Lord and hearing the words, "well done good and faithful servant." Cousin Pam from Indiana sang Mama's favorite song, "Going to Meet the King." I cried a lot. I cried too much. I was all cried out. In a weakened moment with my sentiments, I discussed Mama's last wish with my older brother and sisters—Mark, Frances, and Celia.

"Who's going to take her?" Frances immediately asked, while quickly adding she could not because her job would not allow her to take off any more days. Mark said the trip would be too much for him and his wife and three children. Celia was a crackhead who I wouldn't trust to deliver a bottle of pop next door.

"She asked me," I had said angrily. "I'll do it. I'll take Mama back home by myself."

I would ensure that the body made it to Franklin Memorial Funeral Home in Clayhatchee. I would go down there by myself, have another ceremony with her family, those still living in the cotton belt, and quickly get back to New York. I was resigned to make sure it was done right. That's the least I could do. Mama spoiled me. I was her surprise baby.

Mama was forty when I was born. Daddy was surprised for sure. The last of five children of Elaine and John Kingsman. They named me James after my older brother who died trying to come into this world. Mama proclaimed me the gift, to the chagrin of my siblings. My brother, sisters, and I knew better. Mama was the gift. We owed her everything.

****

The gas station attendant had provided me with perfect directions, and I just followed the signs all the way into Clayhatchee. My family lived on the outer edges of the town just past Hickory Drive. The area still had a rural flavor to it. Germinating from high weeds and wildflowers emerged big old houses with wooden porch swings. However, the country feel—with its holiness and slowness—could not keep city life from creeping in. Across the road from the country homes were MLK Elementary School and then the MLK housing projects (everything seemed to be named for Martin Luther King Jr. in the South).

Slowing down and looking to the rural side of the road, I saw Aunt Dee on her porch. She was shucking green peas. She loomed big, as big as I had remembered, her girth occupying much of the porch swing. As I approached, she seemed to be in thought, in touch, and in tune with herself and the world; humming the old church hymn, "Swing Low, Sweet Chariot."

She looked up and smiled, discarding her pea bowl, and stretching out her arms for me in one impressive motion.

"Is dat you, boy? Dat is you!" said Aunt Dee, as she pulled me to her with kisses, hugs and riotous laughter.

It didn't matter that I was twenty-nine, had been on my own for years, and worked for one of the country's largest newspapers. I was still a boy to her.

I had missed Aunt Dee; I had forgotten how much I loved her. As a child growing up, she visited us often in the summer. Unapologetic about her fear of flying, Aunt Dee made the trek to Pittsburgh on a Greyhound bus. Aunt Dee emerged big. Everything stood big about her—big body, big personality, big voice, and she used her bigness for effect. Her big laugh would have us rolling on the floor. Her big voice with just a hint of anger struck fear in our hearts and trembling to our knees. She was boisterous, unrepentant, and real. She told it like it was. That's probably why she and Daddy got along. She was one of the few people who stood up to him. He liked her for that. Also, Daddy liked that it didn't take much for Aunt Dee to put a switch to us. A woman after his own heart.

"Hey, Aunt Dee," I said as I welcomed her embrace.

"Welcome home, boy," she said squeezing me tighter. "Lets me look at you. James, you grown into a fine-looking man. Sitch down. Sitch down. You hungry?"

I was fourteen the last time I saw Aunt Dee. And although some things might slip a mind in time, I had never forgotten three things about Aunt Dee—her cooking, her belly laugh, and her fondness for using switches on us. Aunt Dee looked old, but it was an unchanged old. She always appeared old to my brother and sisters even when she was in her late forties. Now, in her mid-seventies, her oldness stood justified. I guess that worries from the past—men, children, money, health, life—had taken some shine from her, bent her over a little more, slowed her movement. But she was still Aunt Dee, even as she stood with a cane, walked with a cane, moved with a cane. Diabetes, or sugar as my parents liked to call it, had hit Aunt Dee hard in the last several years. The disease caused the loss of sight in her right eye. With no real purpose, the eye itself had become lazy. Aunt Dee, who had been a hellion, had found God in the last ten years. She worshiped the Lord with as much zest as she did back in the day when she was tearing through juke joints, men, and moonshine. But even as she had gotten right with the Big Man upstairs, Aunt Dee still had a little devil in her.

"Praise be to Gawd dat you made it here safely. Now, what you say you wanted yo Aunt Dee to make fo you?"

"Aunt Dee, I'll eat whatever you make, but let's sit and talk for a while. I want to hear about how you're doing."

We spent the next two hours talking about family—the dead, the married, the jailed, the pregnant, and the divorced.

Aunt Dee was five years older than Mama. From stories passed down, Aunt Dee was fiercely protective of her little sister—fighting boys, threatening fresh old men. Aunt Dee also fought jealous girls and women who thought their men had an eye for Mama. Elaine was a head-turner, after all, so much so that she caught the eyes of many men down in Clayhatchee even as a young girl.

"I knows yo mama was proud of you. How you doin', baby?"

"I'm okay, Aunt Dee. I miss her already. I'm glad, though, I had some time to talk to her. We talked about her life here, and what it was like growing up in Clayhatchee. She told me so much about Pappy and Sugar Mama."

"Pappy and Sugah Mama spoilt yo mama. She was da princess. Did you know yo mama owned a pony? Puddin' was da onliest colored girl wit her own pony."

Pudding is what my mama's people called her back home. Elaine was her fancy uppity northern name.

"Yo mama thought she was sumpin else on dat pony."

We all knew the story about the pony. Daddy called it a mule. He said the mule was nothing much to look at, but the girl on the mule was something else. He would say, "She was the prettiest girl I ever saw, sitting on the ugliest mule I ever saw."

Aunt Dee continued talking about Mama being spoiled, but if anyone spoiled Elaine, it was Aunt Dee. She basically raised Mama.

"Um sorry I couldn't get to yo daddy's funeral," said Aunt Dee. "Musta been rough fo you."

"I mourned for Daddy," I said, "but Mama's death was altogether something different. It seemed much harder to deal with."

Of course, I knew why. Mama wrapped her arms around all of us and loved us and demanded we love each other, and we obliged even when loving felt hard.

"Mama knew love," I continued, "and she knew tenderness."

"Amen, James. Your mama had a true Christian charity about her, not that holy-on-Sunday Christianity."

"Have you ever heard the story of Jughead?" I asked.

"Jughead? No, but tell me."

"Jughead was a white man in his early thirties who used to ride around on a bicycle. Seriously, he was the foulest, nastiest bum in town. One day Mama asked him if he were hungry. He said yes. She fed him."

"Pudding would feed anybody who needed a meal," said Aunt Dee.

"Well, she also asked him if he needed a place to stay and welcomed him into our home. He stayed for six months."

"Lawd," bellowed Aunt Dee.

"One day, when Mama was away doing errands, Daddy had a heart-to-heart with Jughead. When Mama returned, Jughead had moved out. Mama cried. That's just how she was."

"Yo daddy could certainly be persuasive," laughed Aunt Dee.

I laughed with her, which earned me another hug.

The South does call for a slower tempo. I hadn't looked at my watch once, and we hadn't moved from our spot on the front porch since I arrived.

"Boy, when was da last time you had a home-cooked meal? You probably been living on dat fast food mess since you left yo mama's house. Living up in dat New Yoke, I know you haven't had any real down-home food in a long time. Go on upstairs and freshen up. I'll get you some real food."

I walked up the narrow steps. On the walls leading up to the top were family pictures—cousins, aunts, uncles, and my immediate family. There was a black and white picture of my mother with a rag on her head and sandals on her feet. She couldn't have been more than sixteen years old. She was thin and had a slight grin on her face as she tilted her head to the right and placed her hands on her hips. On another wall hung a picture of twenty-something Daddy in his Army uniform holding two fifths in each arm. I couldn't make out the brand of spirits but, if I had to guess, he was probably carrying Canadian Windsor. That whiskey sat on the shelves of our home as long as I could remember. Dad stood tall, thin, and confident with a rare smile on his face. Under that picture was a photo of my siblings in their Sunday best. Frances looked to be six, Mark four, and Cecilia two. I always loved that picture for some reason. Mama had the same picture of those three hanging on our wall at home.

"James, hurry on down fo da food gets cold," Aunt Dee yelled.

"Here I come, Auntie."

I sat down to a spread of fried chicken, black-eyed peas, some collard greens, macaroni and cheese, cornbread, and a large glass of lemonade.

"Aunt Dee, what am I going to do with all of this food?"

"You gonna eat it, boy. You haven't gotten too big dat I can't put a hide to yo butt."

"Oh, please don't. I haven't forgotten the last time you put a hide to me. I like my hide the way it is, bruise-free," I said laughing. "You know they put people in jail for that now."

Aunt Dee replied with her belly laugh.

"My God," I continued, you have enough food here to feed an army."

"First, boy, stop usin' da Lawd's name in vain," she scolded. "You tryin' to get yo butt whopped."

"Sorry, Ma'am. So, how's Bunky these days?"

"You know yo good-fo-nothin' cousin, Bunky, lives down da street now wit his good-fo-nothin' woman."

"Isn't that his wife?"

"Don't interrupt me, chile. She's common-in-law. I guess you can call Gloria his wife if you want to use doze terms. I know he's takin' care of all her children, three with three different men. I told Bunky, I don't know how he's gonna take care of her three children with da two children he has with Lori. Bunky works at da water plant now, and all of his money is going to child support for his own children. Da boy is just hardheaded. He been dat way since he was a chile. I shoulda beat his ass mo."

"Oh, Aunt Dee," I said surprised, but I don't know why.

"Hey, you act like you ain't heard me cuss," she boomed. "I might be a Christian, but I still cuss like a sailor. Pray for me, chile. Bunky should be on his way soon."

CARLISLE

Bunky is Aunt Dee's youngest child. He is five years older than I am, and he's a mess. Bunky is the type of mess that you thought was cool when you were a teenager and you didn't know any better. He made drug-using and selling seem cool. He made juggling four or five girls seem cool, and he made being a teen father seem cool. Aunt Dee called him a thirty-four-year-old wannabe playboy. From talking to him on the phone occasionally, I knew he hadn't moved much beyond adolescence in action and attitude. Bunky still talked junk, and he still spent all his time chasing women. He still slang dope even with his municipal water plant job. And he was still a mama's boy. From what I gathered from Aunt Dee, Bunky stayed right around the corner from her house—close enough to move back in with his mama if his old lady tired of him. It appeared that all my family remained close to home. In fact, two of Aunt Dee's children lived around the block with their grown children.

And they all started to come to see their northern cousin. It did not take long for me to become dizzy with introductions of cousins, aunts, uncles, and friends of the family. A blur of faces, kisses, hugs, and smiles danced in front of me, as people faded in and out all afternoon.

"When you get in, James?" Aunt Earlene asked. Aunt Earlene actually was my cousin, but she seemed so much older I just always called her aunt. She was Aunt Dee's oldest daughter with quite a few years on her younger brother, Bunky. Earlene had to be at least fifty-five now. She gave me a big bear hug, a kiss, and smothered me with her fluffiness. She was round, soft, chocolate, and she had hair on her chest, still. I remember that as a kid when I first saw her. Withstanding her bearded chest, Aunt Earlene still had an attractive face. The rumor was she was fine in her youth, men chasing after her like bees to honey. Today, she was just sweaty with a do-rag on her head.

"Boy, you've gotten so handsome. I'm so sorry about your mama. Pudding was proud of you. J.R. was proud of you too, even if he didn't say so."

J.R. was my father's nickname. I never knew what the R stood for and had never thought to ask, for that matter. Nonetheless, J.R. and Pudding are what their family and friends in Clayhatchee used when referring to them.

"Dat Uncle J.R. and Puddins' youngen?" Cousin Willie asked. "Whad up, bow?"

Seeing my hesitation, Aunt Earlene jumped in.

"Willie said hi," she giggled.

Oh yeah, I remember Cousin Willie. Earlene's oldest child was two years older than his mother's brother, which meant Bunky was Willie's uncle. I never could understand Willie when I was a kid, and nothing had changed. All these relatives were country, but Willie was *country!* Damn.

"Hey, Willie, good to see you," I said, dapping up my cousin.

"Look at you, big-time city reporter," Aunt Earlene continued. "So, are you on television?"

"No, Aunt Earlene. I'm a print journalist. I work for the New York Daily News. I write about politics."

"I guess that's good too," Aunt Earlene said, still smiling or maybe smirking. I couldn't tell.

Whenever someone found out I was a reporter, the first thing they asked me was what television station I was on. Couldn't a brother just write? And the next question was always, do you write about sports? Couldn't a brother write about something other than sports? I was spared from the sports question because at that moment Bunky sauntered into the house, cornrows and all, announcing his arrival.

"Bunky is in the house," he said, kissing relatives as he walked past. Then he saw me. "Is that my little cousin from Pittsburgh? Damn, boy, you ain't so little anymore. In fact, you look a little chubby. Just playing, man. Good to see you. Sorry about the circumstances, but it's damn good to see you again," he said as he pulled me into him. My southern family were huggers.

"He has gotten big," Aunt Earlene said. "James was just a squirt. He has some meat on his bones now, and he's so handsome. Bunky, your cousin was just telling us about his big-time job working for the newspapers."

Bunky stepped back and looked at me. He still had both of his hands on my arms as if to inspect me better and, by the look in his eyes, I knew what he was going to say next.

"What you cover, sports?" Bunky asked. Damn. Really. "Have you

met Michael Jordan? How about Barry Sanders?"
I tried not to roll my eyes, but it was hard.

"I don't cover sports," I said, as I took a seat on Aunt Dee's animal-pattern couch that sagged in the middle. "I cover politics, city council, mayor's office, local government, state, and national elections."

"I guess you haven't met anyone famous," Bunky said with a hint of disappointment in his voice.

"No, I've met plenty of famous people—Bill Clinton, Jesse Jackson, Colin Powell, Mayor Rudy Giuliani." Bunky didn't seem impressed, so I threw in Jamie Foxx, Tisha Campbell, and Ice-T.

"Now you talking, Cuz. Is Tisha as fine in person as she is on TV? That boy Martin Lawrence acted a fool with that girl, driving her from that show. That nigga crazy."

"Hey, hey, hey. I don't wants to hear any of dat, Bunky" Aunt Dee said, leaning forward as if she was going to get up.

"Sorry, Mama. But Tisha is fine."

"Yeah, she is," I said. "In fact, she looks better in person." I missed my days covering entertainment, but politics is exciting in a whole different way.

"Politics," Auntie Earlene said, curling her lip. "I know you keep a headache. You can't trust any of them, Democrats or Republicans. Well, I'm glad to see you. I wish it was under better circumstances, but you're home and your mother's home now too."

"You met Ice-T?" Bunky interrupted. "He's on that show where he plays a cop. How is Ice-T?"

"Ice-T is cool," I said, pun fully intended.

Bunky slapped me on my shoulder.

"We got a regular celebrity in our house, Mama," Bunky said to Aunt Dee.

"Boy, leave dat boy alone," Aunt Dee admonished Bunky, who was grinning widely with a gold tooth in full view.

"Naw, I'm proud of him. I want to show him to the hood," Bunky said, as he turned to me. "Hey, James, you want to take a ride with me? I have to take care of a few things. It won't take long?"

Do I really want to ride with him? Who knows where he's going to take me? I've avoided dives and drug homes since graduating from college. I wasn't being bougie, but I just couldn't think of any other places Bunky would take me. That's my man, but I hadn't forgotten his propensity for the seedy. Well, what the hell.

"Sure, let's ride."

Aunt Dee and Earlene seemed to create a fortress of flesh, flab, and determination in front of the door with matching sets of folding arms and disapproving eyes.

"Bunky, where you takin' James?" Aunt Dee said. "Don't be takin' him through any of doze rough projects and to any of doze hoe-ish girls' houses. In fact, James just arrived. Let him rest awhile fo you start draggin' him all ova town."

"You ain't taking him to any whore houses," Aunt Earlene chimed in.

"Would y'all just chill," a miffed Bunky said. "I got my cousin. Only respectable places."

"I'm fine, ladies." I said.

Bunky turned to his nephew.

"You want to ride, Willie?"

"Na, gawt sum bizness."

Bunky glanced my way.

"If you didn't quite catch his particular dictional flourish," Bunky deadpanned, "Willie said 'no.'"

"Maybe we could get out and see the area where my parents grew up," I said to Bunky. "Mama talked about this place all the time."

"Okay, I guess it will be all right," Aunt Dee interrupted. "Y'all be careful. Take care of yo cousin, Bunky."

"Nuttin' to worry about, Mama. I won't keep him long," said Bunky as we walked out the door with his arm around my shoulders.

Bunky led me to his classic 1994 white Cadillac. I could tell it was his pride and joy by the way he approached it, majestic like. Bunky had the ride souped-up—new stereo system, shiny rims, woofers in the trunk. He put in a Ludacris CD.

"You ready to see the dirty, dirty South?" Bunky asked, as he blasted Ludacris and lit a blunt.

"I'm ready."

Chapter 2
Dirty South

Bunky took me straight to the projects and what the aunts would call "some whorish girl's house." No matter North or South, what city you're in, what town, big or small, projects all look the same. The Martin Luther King Jr. projects in Brooklyn look like the Martin Luther King Jr. projects in Clayhatchee. Imagine that. I had been in quite a few projects myself. I grew up in the projects. I prided myself in the fact I was able to escape the project life, the crime, the drugs, the violence, the baby mama drama; it wasn't easy. You keep in your books. Play sports. Stay out of trouble. Wear a rubber. Bunky told me we were going to see his girl as we pulled up to the housing complex.

"Don't you live with your woman?" I asked.

"Yeah, but I wish I didn't live that close to Mama because Gloria is always telling my business. If I'm late getting home, she is over my mama's house asking if she saw me. That shit gits on a nigga's nerves."

"So, who are you going to see now?"

"I told you, my girl."

"Does she have a name?"

"Wanda."

We walked past a basketball court. Brothers, some looking as if they spent some time pumping iron, were running full court and talking shit to one another. Forty-ounce malt liquor bottles sat next to the fence, close enough to grab during a timeout. We turned into the brick building with a heavy steel door. As always, in projects, there were steps to climb, narrow, dull, gray steps. Among the litter were a couple of spent condoms on the ground. At least someone's practicing safe sex. Nasty. I hadn't been in the projects for some time, but it didn't take long for it all to become familiar again. Oh, yeah, the sweet smell of piss. I don't know why people thought steps in a project building doubled as a toilet. Funky.

"Hey, how many more flights?"

"One more to go. What's the matter, Cuz? Don't y'all exercise up North? If you ain't in shape, I can't hook you up with any of these shawtees. Them southern gals will wear your northern ass out with some of their southern love. You know Frankie Beverly made a song about them. *Southern Gals!*"

Why did I agree to go out with Bunky? I didn't really need to come down South to go to the hood. And Bunky, that brother had a nine to five, his souped-up ride, shacked up with his baby's mama, and his "shawtees" on the side. He was set. The mac daddy of Clayhatchee. I don't know why brothers like Bunky thought this was all they needed in life. They had to see there was more. As we walked through the hallway, we saw two children—couldn't be more than six or seven—running toward us. They bumped into us and kept going.

There was a woman standing outside on her cell phone having a heated discussion with someone. "Beenie, where you at?" she bellowed. "I told you I needed to go to the grocery store. You said you finna be here two hours ago. Where are you? I can't stand triflin' niggas."

We walked two doors from where the woman was arguing with Beenie, and Bunky knocked hard on door five.

"Hey, baby, it's me. Open up," Bunky said, sounding all sweet and a little soft. "It's your boo. Open up."

Wanda, or who I thought was Wanda, swung the door wide open. The grin on her face was as wide as the door was open.

"I didn't know you were coming over. Why didn't you call, baby? I would have had some food ready for you and some other things."

"I want to introduce you to my cousin, James. He's a big-time newspaper reporter from *New Yoke*. He down here for his mama's funeral. You remember I used to tell you about my family up North, Auntie Pudding and Uncle J.R.?"

"Cuz, this is Wanda. Ain't she fine? Go ahead, have a seat. You hungry? You want something to drink? Make yourself comfortable."

Bunky moved around the room as if this were his home. He was comfortable, that's for sure, opening up the refrigerator and pulling out a beer. He sat down in a Lazy-Boy, extended the chair, and promptly threw his left leg over the arm.

"Hi, Wanda. It's nice to meet you," I said, extending my hand to shake hers.

Wanda ignored my hand, bypassed the handshake, and gave me a huge hug.

"If you Bunky's cousin, then we family too," she said.

Wanda wasn't bad. She wasn't fine, but she wasn't bad. And she had back. Southern fried chicken booty. I started humming to myself, LL Cool J's song "Wanda, got a big ole butt." No, it was Brenda's got a big ole butt. Wanda, Brenda. It didn't matter. The girl had a big ole butt on her.

"What you want to drink, Cuz?"

"I'm cool. I'm all right."

"Nigga, don't try to act shy. Wanda, get him one of those cold brews out the *frigidaire*."

Wanda complied. No-fuss. Wanda just dripped in sweetness. There must be something to that southern girl charm. If I had told my girl, Jackie, to serve one of my relatives, she would have looked at me like I was crazy. I could hear her now: "You get it. Nothing's wrong with your feet, and while you're up, get me something."

Don't get me wrong; Jackie was down for me and would do anything for me. She just didn't want me to think so. Northern women were just like that—hard. Their mamas were hard and didn't take any shit from a man, and that's the way their mothers instructed them to be. "Don't let no man push you around. If he's not acting right, you can do bad all by your damn self."

Or you had those sisters who overcompensated because their mothers had been used, abused, and dogged by a man. That would be Jackie. When she was nine, her father left her mother for another woman. He married this other woman, but he kept coming back to Jackie's mother. Every time, he would leave again. Jackie couldn't stand her father for that. She couldn't stand most men for that.

I thought I had broken through her "all-men-ain't-shit" shell. It had been hard as hell to penetrate. Before Jackie, I had been the guy trying to screw every woman I met. But Jackie was smart, funny, cool, sexy, and damn sexy. And I chased her, full sprint. I was in love. I found the one.

She was still looking for the one. But after seven months, she softened, becoming a bit more vulnerable. She told me she loved me. I almost had her convinced that I was her one.

Unfortunately, I hadn't actually turned in my player's card. Not long after Jackie told me she loved me I was out of town covering a story. I finished the story early, went to a bar and met a woman, who was fine by the way. And yes, I found myself extremely attracted to her. And she was throwing everything at me, but unlike the dog of old, I stopped myself. I deflected everything but her phone number, and I felt good about myself. I had no intention of ever calling the woman. Hell, I was proud of myself. I had an opportunity to be a dog, and I decided to be a man. I also realized how deep my feelings were for Jackie. Yeah, she was the one.

I took the number. Big mistake. I kept the number. Bigger mistake. I let Jackie find the number. Biggest mistake.

"Who, the hell is Ce Ce, and what are you doing with her phone number?"

"Well, she...you know when I covered that story. I had to go to New Jersey."

"Why do you have her number, James?"

I really didn't have a good answer. She didn't want to hear how valiant I had been in the face of the booty. Nope. All she wanted to hear now was me dropping my key—her key—on the table. Just like that, we were done. All over my stupidity.

That was about six weeks ago. I hurt so bad I couldn't even summon the dogs. My boys tried to get me out of the house, to the clubs, to play ball. I just wanted to stay home. I didn't even want Ce Ce's number.

When I thought things couldn't get any worse, Mama passed. To her credit, Jackie supported me. Helped me with arrangements. She was a shoulder to cry on. And all that did was confirm what I had thought, she was a damn good woman. She was the one. But it was too late. It was over. The two women who I loved the most were gone from my life. And here I was now, in the projects, drinking a beer with my crazy cousin and Wanda's big ass consuming the room.

"Hey Cuz, do you need another brew? If you need anything, feel free to get it," said Bunky as he walked behind Wanda into her bedroom. Wanda yelled back to ask if I could keep an eye on Little Man, the three-year-old kid who had been preoccupied with the TV. There were four white men on the television dancing and singing, and they all sounded like they were from Crocodile Dundee's neck of the woods. It wasn't James Brown, nor Chuck D, and it wasn't my cup of tea, but the kid seemed to like it. And that was cool with me. Kids and I didn't go. It's not that I didn't like them. I just didn't understand them, and I didn't understand people who wanted to have them. I watched Little Man as he watched TV, and we both drifted—Little Man in song and me in thought.

I again wondered why Mama wanted to come back here, dead or alive. I just didn't see it. And granted, I hadn't made the grand tour, but from the little I saw, Clayhatchee wasn't much. I was with Daddy on this one. Give me the North over the South any day, although I guarantee my daddy wouldn't have gone that far. He always thought southern Black men were a lot smarter, had more know-how, gumption, than any northerner. He pitied me for not growing up on southern soil. I was a Yankee—spoiled by all the convenience and luxuries off the backs of real brave men and women from the South. My father was not a peaceful man, but he praised the courage of the Civil Rights workers who marched in the face of violence and got clubbed as they sat at lunch counters.

"That took bravery," Daddy would say, "bravery you northern Negroes will never know."

"Daddy, you know northerners did go down South to help with the movement?"

"Not enough."

Yep, that was about the stint of our conversation on that matter. Northern brothers had nothing on southern brothers. They could have all of that turn-the-other-cheek mess. Later for that.

If someone was throwing, I was throwing too. I had practiced martial arts since I was twelve, earning a fourth-degree black belt, so I always felt pretty good with my hands and feet. What I was never too good about was turning the other cheek after being slapped. It just wasn't me. Heck, it wasn't my father, so I'm still not sure why he talked about the virtues of the Dr. Martin Luther King Jr. civil disobedience tactics. In an era when Black men hanged freely from trees, justice was a cruel mirage for Negroes, and Jim Crow wouldn't stop crowing, smirking, and snarling. I could never picture my father kowtowing to any white man. John Kingsman saying, "yesump, boss." No, I couldn't see it. My dad was one of those "bad niggers" white people like to call folks who couldn't quite conform to the southern way. In the South, those "bad niggers" didn't last long; dead or jail, most likely dead.

That's probably why my dad left Clayhatchee. That town wasn't big enough for a "bad nigger" like him. His mama, Coco, probably got him out of there before a mob of white people lynched him. He told me how his mother bailed him out of jail when he was a teenager after some racial incident. He was in an ice cream parlor, and a white guy spit in his hair. My dad went to whooping on him, as well as the white boy's four friends. The incident had Daddy in front of some judge.

"You don't have the $130 for the fine," the judge said. "You can spend some time in jail until you get it." According to Daddy's recollection, the judge was smiling.

Daddy said his mama and a friend brought him the money, which he promptly slapped on the judge's bench and walked out of the courtroom. Yeah, I'm sure Daddy had to leave Clayhatchee.

Bunky came out of the room smiling. "You ready to git on out of here?"

"I'm ready."

"Bunky, you and your cousin don't want to stay for dinner? It won't take long for me to fix something," said Wanda, looking and sounding frazzled.

"Naw, baby, we have some things to do. I'll call you later," Bunky said, leaning over to give Wanda a kiss; all tongue, lips, and spit. Yuck.

"Wanda, it was nice meeting you."

"You too, baby. Make sure you come back."

"Well, thank you. Thanks, Little Man, for keeping me company,

CARLISLE

you take it easy," I said to the boy, who was now watching *Dora the Explorer* and still not paying me any attention.

Bunky hurried me out the door, as if he had been waiting on me the entire time. As we made it outside of the projects, I asked him, "what's the rush?"

"Gloria called me three times. I got to get home to the wife and kids. She'll be thrilled to see my big-time *New Yoke* reporter cousin. First, I need to make one more stop."

Gloria and Bunky hadn't officially married, but they had been living together for three years; it seemed legal enough for them. Gloria's three children by three different men was a source of heartburn for Aunt Dee. But Bunky thought of those *other* children as his, and Aunt Dee treated them well even if she didn't care for their mama.

As we rode around my parents' old stomping ground, Bunky blasted some Outkast. Occasionally, Bunky would pull the car over to speak to someone he knew. When we were solidly in the hood, Bunky pulled up next to a group of about four or five hardened brothers, who were just hanging out and gritting their teeth. One looked like a Black Arnold Schwarzenegger; dark-skinned, muscular, and frowning. Another had no business having his shirt off, but he did. Thin, light-skinned, and wearing a red do-rag.

"Y'all seen Bootnanny?" Bunky asked.

None of them said a word. One, however, pointed to a dilapidated house on the corner. Bunky nodded and drove toward the house.

"Chill out here for a second, Cuz. I'll be back in a few minutes."

"You need me to come in with you?"

"No, it's cool. I got some business to handle."

With that, Bunky turned around and walked toward the house. Old discarded wooded stairs with half a banister greeted him, along with a screen door without the screen. A woman came to the door. Frail looking, sickly almost. When she smiled at Bunky, the bareness of her mouth was prominent. She let Bunky in, and he disappeared into the dull gray house.

And I waited.

And I thought.

So on top of being a player, Bunky was a drug dealer too. Oh, if

Aunt Dee knew what her baby boy was up to now. I try not to judge anyone, but I often wondered why Black men, women as well, would demoralize their community with drugs? They would sell drugs to people in their own neighborhoods, have folks they grew up with all cracked out. We contributed to the destruction of our neighborhoods without a thought. Black folks are always talking about the white man, but hell, we do a better job at killing us than the white man has ever done. I wish he would hurry up. I was a bit tired with Bunky's slum tour. Clayhatchee wasn't much. Again, I wondered why Mama was so determined to come back. Come back to what? Projects, hoes, drug dealers, country-as-all-hell-wannabe gang bangers? Mama, I love you. I'm going to do what you asked of me, and then I'm going to hurry my black ass back to New York. Three days. That's it. That's all the time I'm giving. I have to get back.

I was so close to finishing my series about the city's race-based public housing policies. I had worked a straight six months, interviewing, researching, and going on site. All I had to do was to nail down this last main interview with Lamont Bennett. He had been the city's director of Housing and Development until he abruptly resigned three months ago. After months of trying to arrange an interview, he had finally acquiesced, and then Mama passed. If I could just talk to him, I could wrap up the piece and it could run on Sunday. This story was going to shake some folks up. It was going to be my ticket to the big time. I wondered what Jackie was doing.

"Hey, James, you want to see the house your Mama grew up in."

Deep in thought, I hadn't noticed Bunky opening the car door. Bunky lit a cigarette, leaned low in his seat, and pulled off.

"So, do you want to see where Aunt Pudding lived?"

"Sure. Let's go. Am I going to see any more of your girlfriends? Any more projects? Any more hoes? Any more crackheads?"

"I'm offended. I ain't no crack dealer. I just deals in the chronic. I do have hoes all over the place. I ain't saying you won't see another hoe. But, Cuz, we done with the projects and crackheads. I promise." Bunky crossed his heart and cranked up the volume in his system.

So, I was on my way to see where Mama was born. Most folks, Black or white, didn't go to a hospital, to a doctor. They would just have a

CARLISLE

midwife come to their home and help them deliver their babies and keep it moving.

Mama's house was all she knew until she moved to Pittsburgh. She used to tell me how she loved her house. She loved the property more than the house. Her family had owned a little farm. To hear her tell it, it sounded like she had a good childhood. Elaine was spoiled. She was the only colored, that's what they called us then, who had a pony. Her father, Grandpappy, had done well for himself; even in the face of discrimination and racism. And Mama benefited from Grandpappy's success. He doted on her. The old folks say that Mama couldn't do wrong in his eyes.

"Who's the pappy?" Payton Williamson asked, straight-face, no emotions.

The girl didn't answer. She just looked away, and then she looked down, hoping to discover words on the floor that would help wash away, explain away her shame.

"Girl, I said who's that baby's pappy?"

"I don't know, Daddy."

He slapped her across the face, instantaneously regretting what he had just done. But Payton Williamson was not going to let up even as his baby girl started to cry, not noticeably but enough for him to be pained. He had to make things right for his Elaine, even if it meant inflicting some pain on her. John Kingsman had to do right by his daughter—that was that.

"Bring that no-good son of a bitch Kingsman to me. Go fetch him. Tell him I want to see him."

"No, Daddy, don't have him come here. Please."

"What do you think?" Bunky asked.

"Think about what?"

"This is your Mama's old house."

All I saw was mostly barren land. Looked like it had been scorched. I couldn't believe anything had lived, thrived, let alone, survived on this property; filled with rocks, weeds, empty beer bottles, and other debris of neglect. The property was not as big as Mama made it out to be. She had described it as a glorious place where she roamed free. Time has a way of doing that to our memories. A bedraggled structure barely stood near the far end of the lot. It looked too tiny to have accommodated a family with six children. The roof of tar and shingles had caved in. The structure tilted to the left side, as if it were trying to disconnect itself from its roots.

"Was that her house? And what happened to it?"

"That's it, Cuz. The land and the house had been torched in the 1940s by some Klan. Our grandpappy barely got out of there alive."

"So, why did they torch it?"

"Why did the Klan ever do anything? They wanted to frighten niggers."

"It has to be more to the story than that. There had to be more of a reason."

"Y'all northern cats always think there has to be a reason for white folks killin', scarin', or hurtin' niggas.

The reason is always the same. They did it because they could. And here's another thing for you, Cuz. Don't think the killin', scarin', and hurtin' have stopped because it's the twenty-first century. Cuz, you still needs to be careful in these parts. That's real talk."

"So, Grandpappy never rebuilt?"

"Naw, he lost everything. He had to go sharecrop on old Wayman's property for the rest of his life. Truth be told, Mr. Wayman was a good cracker, according to my mama, but Grandpappy never got over losing his property. He died a bitter old man. You don't remember Grandpappy; he was an evil old man. Beat you for looking the wrong way."

Mama hadn't told me that the house had been burned down. I wondered why she never said anything. All of her stories about this place were fabulous. The property, the magnificent home. She had been proud of her dad. He had done something many Blacks here hadn't done at that time. He had managed to work hard, save money, and bought his own property. He worked the land for himself. He stressed to all of his children that they needed to do for themselves. According to Mama, her daddy was a Booker T. Washington man—you know, do for yourself, pull yourself up by your own bootstraps, cast down your bucket where you are. Booker T. Washington saw the need for Black people to not only learn a craft but to own their own land and businesses. They needed to be entrepreneurs. Grandpappy bought in completely to what Booker T. Washington was selling. Mama told me that Grandpappy would always say, "No need to go with your hat in your hand asking the white man for anything because he's never going to give you what you want or deserve." That was pretty radical thinking back then. Mama never described Grandpappy as militant but did say he was proud. It's a shame. In the end, he had to go to the white man with his hat in his hand to help him take care of his family. That's some tragically ironic shit.

I wondered what stories were still on this land and what I would miss and what my children (the ones I'm not having) would miss. What secrets did this house carry for my mother?

****

Bunky must have forgotten that he had to quickly get home to Gloria and the three kids. Instead, he stopped at his Mama's home. As soon as we entered the door, Aunt Dee fussed at Bunky and me. She mostly fussed at Bunky, telling me not to let her no-good-for-nothing son get me into any trouble. Reminding me that I was a good boy trying to do things with my life, while all Bunky wanted to do was chase women, hang out all night, and "drink that malt liquor mess." Bunky hugged Aunt Dee in an effort to slow down the assault and to maneuver his way out of the door. On his way out, Bunky asked me if I wanted to come to his house to meet Gloria and the kids. I had enough cousin time for one night. I told him I was tired, and he told me to get my rest because there was lot more left on the Bunky dirty, dirty South tour.

Rest was exactly what I needed, but I forced myself to do some work. All I wanted was to get that last interview. New York was an hour ahead, already 10 p.m. I could call Bennett on his cell phone, but it might be too late. I hated bothering people. I always hated that part of my job. The nagging. The chasing. The calling. The bothering. And at the *New York Daily* you hadn't done your job if you hadn't called an individual ten or twelve times at the office, six or seven times at home, physically gone to the office and sat and waited for two or three hours, and lastly gone to the person's home, and surprised the hell out of an unexpected spouse or child, as well as the person you've been hunting down all day. Oh, I hated that. It really wasn't in my nature. Yet, I could turn on the aggression, be dogged in the pursuit of a story. But I had to transform myself into that—step out of my shy inner self and become a pain in the ass. I guess it was time to become a pain in the ass.

I whipped out my cell phone, pulled out Bennett's number from my briefcase. I dialed and waited, and waited, and waited, and waited, and waited, and then I heard, "The customer you've reached is unavailable." I tossed the phone on the dresser in what used to be Bunky's room. I'm sure he'll find his way back here again.

Where are you, Bennett? You told me that I could always reach you on this phone. I wonder if he's screening his calls. You're holding up my story, man. I laid across the bed, plotting. I'll call his law office first thing in the morning. That's what I'll do. I still have time.

Aunt Dee had placed a towel and washcloth on my bed. After I showered, I thought about reading, but hadn't realized how much the drive had worn me out. And spending all that time with Bunky didn't provide much rest. I went downstairs to tell Aunt Dee goodnight, hearing what I knew was wrestling on the television. When I was a kid and Aunt Dee would visit, she kept our TV on wrestling every night, much to Daddy's amusement and Mama's abhorrence. "Dee, isn't there anything else you can watch than those half-naked men, grunting and sweating?"

"Das why I watch em, Puddin' ... dey half-naked, dey gruntin', and dey sweaty," she would say with a belly laugh.

When I went downstairs, wrestling was on, but Aunt Dee wasn't watching. She was sitting in her rocking chair going through some old pictures and crying softly. Aunt Dee was drinking out of a mayonnaise jar. I recognized the smell of rum in a jar.

I put my hand on Aunt Dee's shoulder.

CARLISLE

"You okay, Auntie?"

"James, I miss yo mama sumpin fierce. I feel like dey just a big hole in my heart. I knows it was Gawd's time fo her. It was Gawd's plan. But I still miss her. Yo mama was a beautiful woman, a good woman, a Gawd-fearin' woman. I wish we had spent mo time together in deze lass years. I shoulda made another trip up noath. A lot of unfinished business."

Aunt Dee seemed to go somewhere else. She seemed to forget I was still there.

"Chile, so much unfinished business," Aunt Dee repeated as she rocked faster back and forth in her chair and stared into space.

"What do you mean, Auntie? What unfinished business?"

My question brought her back, and she looked me in the face. The crying stopped and a calmness came over her as if she were trying to reassure me of something.

"James, some things, I guess, are best left unfinished. Some things are best left buried," she said in a way to tell me she was done discussing this matter. And now, she had me wondering.

Was Aunt Dee losing her mind? I know she and Mama were close, but Mama's passing wasn't a surprise. Mama had been sick for some time. They had said what they needed to say to each other. Hadn't they? I had been home in Pittsburgh because Mama didn't have much longer. I know about a week before Mama died that she and Aunt Dee had talked on the phone for hours. And I remember that because Mama had been so sick that she hadn't spent more than ten or fifteen minutes talking to anyone; phone or in person. I also remember that conversation because it involved a lot of whispering, a lot of crying, a lot of praying. I'm not sure, though, if that two-hour phone call had provided relief or closure for Mama or Aunt Dee. Mama did have a resolute look on her face when she finished the call. I also remember that conversation for one more thing—that's the first time she told me she wanted to be buried in Clayhatchee and she wanted me to make sure it was done.

"What Mama, you don't want to be buried in Oakhart Cemetery with Daddy?"

"I'll be with your daddy in Glory."

"You really think so? I mean, I know you'll be there."

"Yes, I plan on seeing your daddy in Glory, but I want my body to be buried in Clayhatchee, at home. Will you promise me that, James?"

"If that's what you want, Mama, that's what we'll do."

I remember thinking what a strange request. She had lived all her life with this man, and, in death, she wanted to be hundreds of miles away from him. But I guess only the bodies would be separated and not the spirits. At least that's what Mama said. But I wasn't as convinced as Mama that Daddy had made it to the top floor, or the middle floor for that matter. Mark, Frances, or Celia could not believe that Mama wanted to be buried in Clayhatchee. In fact, Frances all but called me a liar. She asked me why Mama would want to leave Daddy, her church people, her family, and friends, to rest eternally in Clayhatchee. Frances also informed me that there would be no one to visit Mama's grave, except for Aunt Dee, who wouldn't be around for much longer. What then? They wanted to know when Mama said it. Who else was around? Apparently, I had been the only family member she had informed of her wishes. Well, lucky for me, Mama wrote her wishes in her diary. If not for the diary, it would have gotten ugly with my siblings, especially with Frances.

Why did everything have to be a battle with my family? We were always bickering, especially me and Frances. Because she was the oldest, Frances thought she had to be a mother as well as a big sister. Mama saved me from her wrath on several occasions, and Frances was convinced I was spoiled because of Mama's protection. Yes, our parents had mellowed somewhat by the time I came through, but it was never a picnic in John Kingsman's house.

Before I left, Frances had the nerve to tell me to bring back anything and everything that I found that belonged to Mama and Daddy. "Don't be picking and choosing, so you can get the best things. Bring it all back, so we all have the opportunity for some keepsakes."

To that, I think I told Frances she could kiss my ass, my entire ass. With Daddy gone and now Mama, there was no need for me to ever go back to Pittsburgh. I was done with those folks. Yeah, Mama kept the family together. With her gone, it didn't seem like much of a family at all.

CARLISLE

"Goodnight, Aunt Dee. You need to get some sleep yourself. Tomorrow is going to be a big day. We'll have to make the final arrangements. Mama's body should have gone straight to the funeral home. I'll call in the morning to make sure everything is okay."

That's not the only place I needed to call. Aunt Dee hadn't said anything to me as I went upstairs. She was holding a picture in her hand. It was a picture of a baby. I couldn't tell if it was a boy or girl, but the baby looked white. With an old black and white picture, it was hard to tell, though. Well, no time to dwell on that. I needed to get some sleep. I had to call Bennett, then the funeral home, and I might call Jackie. Who was I kidding? I was going to call Jackie first.

Chapter 3
The Benefactor

"Hey, baby. It's me. How are you doing?"
"James, is everything okay?"
"Yeah, everything is good. Did I wake you, Jackie? I'm sorry."
"Don't worry about it. It was time for me to get up. How's everything working out for you? Have you finalized your plans for your mother? How are you holding up?"
"I'm doing fine. I should have everything finalized today, and tomorrow we will have the service. I might drive home right after the service. I need to get back. I have so much work to do still."
"Why are you even worrying about that, James? The only thing you need to concentrate on is your mother's last wish. That work will be there when you get back. No need to rush back into it. You just lost your mother. You need to take some time to mourn and reflect."
"I've already mourned, baby. I'm ready to get back. There's nothing here. This is not my home. It hasn't been Mama's home for fifty years. I'll never understand why she wanted to come back here. I don't see it. Everything I need is in New York. Do you understand, Jackie? Everything that I want and need is in New York. You think that maybe we could..."
Ah. Too soon. Why do I always push things?
"James, we'll talk later. I really have to get ready for work now. Hey, keep your eyes open. You might end up seeing what your mother saw there. I'll talk to you later. Have a safe trip home. And James, I'm really sorry about your mother. She was a wonderful woman."
With that, Jackie hung up the phone, not waiting for me to say

CARLISLE

goodbye. At least we talked. Before Mama got sick, Jackie wasn't even picking up her telephone. It's funny it took my mother for her to at least start speaking to me again. I guess that's fitting. She loved Mama and Mama loved her. Mama told me I needed to latch onto Jackie and keep her. And Mama didn't warm up to many of my girlfriends. That just wasn't her. However, the strangest thing happened when she met Jackie—she hugged her with a long knowing embrace. Tripped me out. Mama told me later she just knew about this one, and her feeling was confirmed by the way I looked at Jackie. She said I had the look of a man in love; a look that was fierce, brazen, and unafraid. She said I had murderous eyes. Mama said she knew those eyes—Daddy had them. Mama knew. I knew too. I knew I had to get back to my girl. I had to wrap up this business and hurry back to make things right with Jackie.

* * * *

What a lovely funeral home, if one can consider such a place lovely. Remove the sign in the front, you wouldn't know this was a resting place for the dead. It looked like someone's house, furbished with a porch swing. The white swing greeted mourners before they entered into the lobby. Also, a wooden fence went around the funeral home. It was all too quaint. Franklin Memorial Funeral Home had been taking care of Black folks from Clayhatchee since the 1920s. I'm sure the place helped to bury its share from my family tree. The business had survived Black Tuesday and the rest of the Depression. But why wouldn't it? Death, no matter what the market did, never had an off year, especially in Black communities. And in the South, I'm sure the Klan helped contribute to the funeral home's prosperity. I'm sure brothers have also kept this place busy—Friday night shootings, Saturday night stabbings, and Sunday morning services. Yeah, the Franklin Memorial Funeral Home never had to worry about lacking Black customers.

The Franklins had become a respected family in these parts. Aunt Dee said the funeral home never had any problems with the town's white residents. Franklin's business ensured segregation in death.

Also, when bodies were coming home during World War II, white funeral homes couldn't handle the traffic. Sylvester Franklin dressed and fixed those young white soldiers up like they were royalty and charged their families half as much as they would have been charged at a white funeral home. White folks didn't forget Franklin's work during that period, and the funeral home had a friend in the white establishment as long as it didn't become one of those civil rights agitators. Unbeknownst to Clayhatchee's white power brokers, Sylvester Franklin for years secretly had put money behind the civil rights movement and was a major sponsor of the NAACP. The funeral home stood as a pillar in the Black community.

Sylvester Franklin IV opened the door and greeted me.

"Mr. Kingsman, I presume. Sylvester Franklin. Come on in. It's nice to finally meet you in person. With our several conversations on the phone, I feel like I already know you," the portly funeral home director said. He looked almost as I had expected. He was a dark brown-skinned man, round, jovial, and in his fifties. He extended a chubby hand to me and pumped mine with vigor, smiling widely the entire time. He instantly put me at ease.

"Your funeral home looks so homey," I said.

"Well, thank you, Mr. Kingsman. That's the feel and look we are trying to go for. We want people to feel comfortable coming in here. It shouldn't be a scary or depressing place. My hope, which was the same for my daddy's and granddaddy's, is that when people see this place, they realize that we are going to take good care of them and their loved ones. It puts people at peace, at ease."

"Mission accomplished. So, what's the game plan, Mr. Franklin?"

"We'll have the viewing tomorrow at 11 a.m. and we will then start the service at 1 o'clock. After the funeral, we will go to Hallas Park for your mother's final resting place. I've already put the notice in the local paper."

"Oh, okay, that's good. So, Mr. Franklin, how much is all of this going to cost?"

"There's no cost to you and your family, Mr. Kingsman."

"No cost? Did my mother's insurance company pay you directly?"

"The tab has been picked up by a prominent citizen in this

community."

"Really? Well, who is it, so I can thank that person."

"I'm sorry, Mr. Kingsman, but I can't divulge that information. The person wishes to remain anonymous."

"Really? Do you know why?"

"No, I don't, Mr. Kingsman, and I didn't ask any questions. I just thought of it as a generous blessing to your family."

My siblings would certainly be happy they wouldn't be dividing the funeral cost, especially evil-ass Frances.

"Well, can you tell me anything about this person? One thing?"

"The benefactor is white."

White? What white person did my mama know down here? My parents did not socialize with a lot of white folks in Pittsburgh. There were two families of white neighbors, and we played with their children while growing up. And it took years of cultivation and knocking down some cultural barriers, particularly for my father, to allow friendships to blossom between us and each of those two families. So, what white person, family, people in the South had been so close to my mother, father, family that they would foot the bill? I understood the person's right to privacy, but I wanted to know. And the more I thought about it, the more I thought I had the right to know.

"Is there anything else you can tell me about the donor, Mr. Franklin?"

"The donor also wanted me to inform you that all of your bills will also be paid—flight, travel, food, etc. All you have to do is submit a list of your expenses to me. I'll make sure it gets to the benefactor."

"You must be joking. This is unbelievable. I drove, and I'm staying with my aunt, so I don't have a lot of expenses."

"No joke, Mr. Kingsman. Just get me an expense list, and I'll make sure you are reimbursed before you leave Clayhatchee. Would you like to see your mother right now?"

I couldn't help but think of this mysterious donor as I followed Mr. Franklin into another room, where Mama laid in her eternal state. She looked peaceful. I know people always say that of the dead, but it was true. She had a good life, as good of a life that could be expected of a Black woman growing up in America. It was not always easy, particularly in the first part of the twentieth century. She had to face life as a Black woman in a society that didn't see much value in her, her potential, her future. She was dominated by Black men, desired and marginalized by white men, hated and mammified by white women. Mama raised four children, worked as a housewife, with no time-off, few benefits, no sick days or vacations, and no union. But she was a dedicated worker, devoted to her job of caring for a husband, who could be surly, and children who could be ungrateful. And Mama probably thought her job would become easier as her children grew into adulthood. No, that wasn't the case. She still played mama to adults who made wrong choices, made mistakes, who still needed that outwardly exhibition of love. She worked hard and long. It was time for her to rest and her rest looked peaceful, and for that I was glad.

Mama loved flowers. She would have enjoyed this spread. Bouquets of flowers to include red roses, white carnations, blue anemones, red amaryllises, yellow chrysanthemums, and white orchids adorned her resting corner. I was blown away. I did not think Mama still had many connections, friendships here in Clayhatchee. She had been gone for more than a half-century. Surely most of these flowers had to be family. I began reading through the cards attached to the flower display. Oh, yes, a lot of families had sent flowers. That's what they do in the South. Not to say flowers aren't important in the North, but I think for southerners, the more flowers surrounding a casket, means the more loved that person was. Mama was like that. Anytime someone died, she made sure we sent flowers, even if we barely knew the person.

Mama would have been mighty proud of this display, wall-to-wall flowers. I had ordered an arrangement of two dozen roses—red, white, pink, and yellow. And as spectacular as my arrangement was, it couldn't hold a candle to the arrangement at the front of the casket. It almost appeared to fan out and around the top of the casket, providing my mother a splash of dazzling colors and royal appearance. The splendor of the display almost kept me from noticing the gold card. I grabbed the card, which read:

"I hope you find the peace you've search for all of your life. Your search is over. M."

The person signed the card with the letter M. No first name, no last name, and not even two initials. Just M. Another mystery. I wondered if M had any connections to the family's generous donor. I sought out Mr. Franklin, who was busy with another family; two elderly white women. They were trying to make arrangements for a young man, a son of one of the women, who recently died in a house fire. They had asked for a closed casket. I could wait.

As I walked near the long back table, I noticed the programs for Mama's funeral. Aunt Dee's pastor was performing the service and some of her church members from Mount Zion Baptist Church were going to sing. I saw my name on the program. I knew I was going to be speaking, but I hadn't prepared much for it. All I needed was a little time and space, and I could come up with the right words about Mama. That would not be hard. Not hard at all.

Mr. Franklin walked toward me after he finished with the women. Even round and jovial, he was a handsome man with reticent charm. Although polite, he was extremely reserved in his approach, but comforting at the same time.

"Is there anything else that I can do for you, Mr. Kingsman?"

"Well, do you know who sent these flowers, signed M?"

"They're from your donor."

Mr. Franklin could have been a reporter the way he protected the name of his source. He didn't even tip me off to the benefactor being a man or woman. For the world of me, I just couldn't figure out why would some white person pay for all of Mama's funeral expenses and my expenses as well? Who was this person? The journalist in me started to kick in, edging out my desire to quickly return to New York. My curiosity was nudging me to dig deeper, but that feeling was fleeting. What did it matter?

No, I had no time to be monkeying around with this mess. The sooner Mama was laid to rest, the sooner I would be back home.

I wondered if Aunt Dee knew anything about the mystery white donor.

Chapter 4
Shadows

"What a pretty Negress you are. You look like one of those mulattoes, but I know you ain't. I done seen your parents, and they two niggers to the bone. How you become so light-skinned with them darkies as parents? Huh, girl? Do you hear me speaking to you?"
"What do you want with me, Mr. Red?"
"I just want conversation, dat's all. I just think you a pretty little Negress. Dat's all. Are you scared of me? Don't be. I won't hurt you."
"Mr. Red, I gots to get home, my pappy and mama going to be looking for me."
"Well, you don't wanna keep your mammy and pappy waiting. You go on and gets. I'll be seeing you again. I'm sure of it."
The young girl ran as fast as she could.

The next morning, the day of my mother's going home ceremony, I arose early to take a jog. I hadn't run since I left New York. It felt good to get out of the house to clear my mind. I had some lingering unease about the M donor that I pushed to the back of my mind to prepare for the service and my return to New York. I had run farther than my customary two miles. I was in a groove. I was in thought. I was feeling happy when I realized I had already been running for an hour and needed to turn around and head back to my aunt's house. When I finally reached Aunt Dee's, my shirt was soaked, my legs were screaming, my lungs felt raw. As I walked into the door, I yelled for Aunt Dee. She didn't answer. Normally, she was sitting in her recliner watching television. If not there, she was cooking in the kitchen. I hadn't smelled any pork when I walked into the house, so she must not be in the kitchen. I yelled again.

"Chile, why all da yelling? I'm upstairs getting' ready fo da service, and I suggest you do da same. We needs to get dere early. You need to be dere and greet folks, James."

"Aunt Dee, can I come up and talk to you?"

"Alright, chile, but be quick. We don't have a lot of time and you still has to get in da shower."

When I walked into the room, Aunt Dee was fully dressed and ready to go. Sitting on the edge of her bed, she flipped through a tattered photo album, staring at pictures of her and my mama when they were young. On the nightstand were spent tissue papers.

"Yo mama sure was a pretty woman, James. Look at dis picture. Dis picture here is from 1946 at da county fair. We both thought we was cute. I think it was at dis fair dat yo daddy got his first good look at yo mama. You know dat look when men finally open dey eyes and see what's in front of dem. After dat, he was like a bee buzzin' round lookin' to taste yo mama's honey." At that, she chuckled to herself.

"Old John Kingsman did some courting," I said. "I'm sure that was a sight to see."

"Oh, he came round Daddy's house wit his hat in his hand, tryin' to win yo grandparents' approval. Daddy didn't like him much. He thought yo daddy was too wild. Daddy said some white men was goin' to end up killin' John cause of his prideful ways. Even though Daddy didn't care too much bout John, he respected him. But Daddy was worried dat John's boldness wit white folks would lead to some bad times for his baby girl."

"Could you blame Granddaddy? I would have been concerned if John Kingsman wanted to court my daughter."

Aunt Dee picked up another picture and started smiling. It was a picture of Mama, Daddy, Aunt Dee, her first husband, Roy, and two or three other couples sitting around a table full of whiskey bottles and lit cigarettes. They all looked so young, so happy.

"Yo daddy begged my daddy to have yo mama's hand in marriage.

41

J.R. told my daddy dat he would protect her with his life. Dat he would love Puddin' all of dere days, and he would neva let nothin' bad happen to her. I heard it all. Made me cry. But you know what? Daddy still said no. It wasn't until ..." Aunt Dee stopped in mid-sentence and looked around.

"It wasn't until what, Auntie?"

"Well, Daddy got to know de true John Kingsman, an afta finally warmin' up to him, gave his blessing."

"Well, I guess Daddy had a little charm in him after all. Hey, Aunt Dee, something kind of strange and unexpected happened. Someone paid for all of Mama's funeral expenses. Even crazier, someone wants to pay for all my expenses. And, the donor doesn't want to be identified. Do you have any idea who would be so generous and why?"

"No chile. But what a wonderful thing. A lot of people loved yo mama. Even though she had been gone for all dat time, yo mama left a lot of friends an family back here. No telling who would do such a thing. But I just think it's God's work. Yo mama was one of His, and He's still takin' care of her and her family. What a blessing. I wouldn't worry too much bout it. Just accept it for what it is—a blessing, pure and simple."

"Well, Aunt Dee, let me ask you this. Who would sign a card with M?"

"M? What you talkin' bout, boy?"

"The largest and probably the most expensive arrangement of flowers came from a person who just signed the card M. Mr. Franklin confirmed that M was the benefactor. Do you know any M's who would have the money and desire to foot the bill?"

Aunt Dee mechanically placed the photo album back on her nightstand as she looked beyond me.

"James, it's no tellin'. M fo mystery. I guess you should just take dis blessing an be happy. Go on now, chile. You need to get ready."

"Dee, I'm scared. I don't know what to do. Mr. Red won't leave me alone."

"Mr. Red? What's dat peckerwood doing? Did he put his hands on you?"

"No, he hasn't. But he's been real familiar. Every time he sees me, he wants to talk to me, saying I'm pretty, the prettiest dark meat in all of Clayhatchee."

"Dat damn white trash. He has a wife. A good wife, and he's trying to chase after some girl? Just tell him thank you and keep on movin'."

"Dee, it's more den dat. It's more den a compliment. Dat man frightens me."

"You want me to say sumpin to Daddy?"

"No, I don't want to get Daddy in any trouble with these white folks."

"Well, you want to say sumpin to John?"

"Dee, c'mon, that's even worse. You want to get John put in jail or killed? You know John won't let this stand. And dese white folk just need the slightest reason to put a rope around his neck.

I'll handle dis myself."

"No, you're not going to handle dis yoself. You'll have me and my Smith and Weston. No mo walkin' round by yourself. Just stay as far away from Red Mansfield as you can. You hear?"

"I hear."

Chapter 5
The Woman in Black

Aunt Dee and I greeted folks as they filed into the funeral home. I didn't realize how much family the Kingsmans had left in the South. And I'm not just talking Clayhatchee. Relatives from Mississippi, Georgia, North Carolina, South Carolina, and Tennessee all made the sojourn to say goodbye to Elaine Kingsman. They were all my people. My family, all different colors and hues. Some folks I remembered vaguely from them visiting my home, years earlier, like Cousin Jenny. I couldn't forget Cousin Jenny. I may have been a young boy, but I noticed how magnificently beautiful she appeared. Perfect, flawless brown skin, the color of caramel. She had a round, pie face, with large bright lively eyes. Now in her early fifties, her beauty had not diminished a bit. To my delight, Cousin Jenny recognized me immediately.

"James, look at you. You're a full-grown man. I can't believe it's you," she said, hugging me tightly. "You were a skinny little thing. You've grown into a man."

"Hey, Cousin Jenny. How have you been?"

"I can't complain. All my children are grown and out of the house. Do you remember Beannie? She's in her last year of college. Can you believe it? My baby's going to be a teacher.."

"How's Roger and Dianne?"

"Both of them are married now with children of their own. I have four grandchildren. Roger owns his own business. He sells computers. Dianne is a stay-at-home mother. Her husband's an engineer, and they live in a beautiful home in Atlanta. So, what are you doing with yourself these days?"

CARLISLE

"I'm a writer. I work for the *New York Daily News*. I've been there for two years now."

"Oh, my goodness. The *New York Daily News*. I'm so proud of you. I know your mama and daddy were proud too. How are you doing? How's the rest of the clan doing up North?"

"I'm hanging in there, Cousin Jenny. And everyone else is doing well. We all had a chance to tell Mama goodbye because of the length of her sickness. The strange part about everything is that we all had lengthy talks with her, and I was the only one she directly asked to have her buried in Clayhatchee. I still haven't figured that out."

"Well, James some things shouldn't be figured out. They should just be done by a leap of faith. Your mama had an abundance of faith. She had faith in John that he would take care of her and all of her children. She had faith in a better life up North. She had faith in God and His blessing on her life. And she had faith the South would welcome her back, as it has. Most importantly, she had faith that you, her baby son, would do what he promised and bring her back home. Her faith was well placed."

That hit me somewhere deep, bringing with it tears that had been too stubborn to face since arriving in Clayhatchee. Cousin Jenny wrapped me up in her arms. I felt five again.

"I miss her."

"I know you do. We all do. But everything is going to be alright. You'll see. Your mama's at peace, and you're a big part of that, James."

With that, Cousin Jenny left. And I was again shaking hands with relatives who I barely knew. Aunt Dee was smiling, looking at all the flowers that had made it to the funeral home. Just like Mama, I thought.

"Oh, yo mama would be so happy with this turnout. All da flowers are beautiful," Aunt Dee said, looking upon the arrangement proudly. "I sure hope I get half these flowers when da Good Lawd calls me home."

"Aunt Dee, you're going to live forever. No time to be worried about funeral flowers."

"James, no one lives on dis earth forever. But dere sure is a place up yonder for Gawd's people. Yo mama's dere now, an she's smilin'."

45

"I hope she is."

"She is."

A lovely, older white woman walked up to Mama's casket. She wore a stylish hat that women wear to church on an Easter morning—except it was black. And black was her color. Yes, others had on black, but she wore it; she brought a bit of regality to the event, even in the way she dabbed her eyes with a black handkerchief. She stayed at the casket longer than other folks, and it appeared as if she was saying something. I couldn't make out what it was. I found myself walking toward her. I had to talk to her. I had to know what she had whispered to Mama. I had to know who she was. As I moved toward my mama's casket and the woman in black, Pastor K. Williams motioned it was time for the service to start. Aunt Dee motioned me to the front row to take my place of honor.

Williams preached about the afterlife; about Sister Elaine coming home, about her faith. He knew a lot about Mama. I guess Aunt Dee had told the reverend of Mama's many years as a member of the First Baptist Church in Homewood. And I heard some "Amens" and "Yes Lord's," some "Hallelujah's" and so much crying. But beyond those things, I didn't hear much of the sermon at all. I was preoccupied with that particular stranger in black. I mean, I knew her as well as I knew the rest of these people, which was not well at all, but something about her stood out. There was something familiar about the lady in black. I tried to focus on where she was, so I could go to her immediately after the funeral. I glanced back, and there she was in the last row in the seat closest to the door. I wonder if she was my M? No, I had convinced myself M was some rich cat; some old rich brother who made it good in business or some other professional field, who carried a torch for Mama all these years. The guy was heartbroken that he would never be able to reconcile his love for Elaine. I don't know. My mind was racing. If I didn't find out who M was by the end of today, I probably wouldn't. It was back to New York tomorrow. Back to reality.

Aunt Dee slowly carried herself and her weight to the front of the funeral home. She always walked with a shuffle, which had become noticeably slower than what I remembered as a child. Aunt Dee went straight into telling stories of their youth and how pretty her sister was, and how that beauty stayed with her throughout her life, growing bigger from the inside and out. Oh, yes, how her sister was a child of God. Members of the pastor's church sang "His Eye is on the Sparrow," and that brought a fresh round of tears. And now it was my turn to speak.

"We are now going to hear a few words from Elaine's son, James," Rev. Williams said, as he nodded my way. "He's a good young man, fulfilling his mama's last wish to be buried at home, the home of so many who shed their blood, who worked the cotton fields, who sang spirituals and toiled in the sun for so long, so many who walked on the front for our rights, so many soldiers. Well, we have another soldier coming home. Elaine wanted to be home and her son made it happen. C'mon up, James."

I slowly got up from the chair, not sure what I would say. I had put some words down on a piece of paper, but they didn't seem like enough. What words could I use to sum up her existence, to express what she meant to me and what she meant to others? When I reached the podium and leaned into the mic, the words came to me.

"My mama never stopped thinking of this place as home. She loved it. Even after fifty-four years in Pittsburgh, Clayhatchee was her home, and she never let us forget. However, it was not until her final days that she really shared with us why she was still connected to this place. I knew she had family. I knew she still had friends here, but she had something else here. Mama told me part of her spirit was here. Fertilized here. Left here to grow. She said that although she lived in the North, her heart would always remain here in the South. She wanted to be home. Mama, you're home now."

I hunched over the podium, trying to fight back tears in vain.

"It's okay, James, take yo time," Aunt Dee said with her eyes closed, rocking back and forth in her chair.

"I hope Mama has found what she wanted to find," I continued. "I hope she's at peace now."

I sat down and Rev. Williams finished the funeral with a prayer and a calling to be saved. Two people accepted the Lord on Mama's second funeral day. Mr. Franklin gave the instructions to take one more look at Elaine Kingsman before she went to her final resting place.

Elaine was to be buried with her father and mother in the Cedar Hill Cemetery. Aunt Dee said she had a spot prepared right next to her younger sister when her time came, ensuring none of them would be alone. As I went up to take my last look of my mother, I searched the back row for the woman in black. She was still sitting there. I caught myself staring at her, her narrow nose, fair skin, long hair. Again, I sensed something strangely familiar about her. I looked at my mother. I quickly looked back up at the woman in black to see if I were losing my mind or something, but she was gone. Yeah, I was probably losing my mind, and the process had started a while back.

I rushed outside and didn't see her. She had disappeared. But, across the street, oddly enough, stood an elderly white man. He had to be in his late 80s. The man was bent over a bit but appeared defiant with frown lines throughout his face. His hair was white and sparse, allowing for a view of his skull. He propped himself up with the use of a brown wooden cane. The scowl on is face looked as if he wanted to beat the hell out of Father Time for making him so damn old. And he was staring. At me? Yes, I believe, he was staring at me. But before I could fully confirm if I were the target of his scowl, several Black folks came out of the funeral home staring and pointing at the old man.

"Is that Red Mansfield? Lord, I thought he was dead years ago," a woman said.

"He probably is dead and dat's his ghost," another lady said, laughing.

Aunt Dee tapped me on the shoulder and told me Bunky and four of his friends were ready to carry Mama's casket into the hearse. She told me I needed to go back inside and find Mr. Franklin. She also told me the vehicles for the procession were beginning to line up and we would ride in Earlene's car in the front. Suddenly, she stopped talking, her face almost as white as the old man still standing across the street. Aunt Dee gripped my arm and pulled me back into the funeral home. I swear that old white man, who had been dour-looking the entire time, smiled at me. Or was it a smirk?

"Whoa, slow up, Auntie, no need to drag me. I'm coming," I said, as I followed Aunt Dee back into the funeral home.

"Dere goes Mr. Franklin. Go see him. He'll tell you what you have

CARLISLE

to do. Go on, son."

    I walked over to Mr. Franklin. He led me to the room where Bunky and his Dirty South crew were waiting. We picked up Mama's casket, three to each side, and put it in the hearse. Mama was making her last trip through Clayhatchee.

Chapter 6
An Unspeakable Horror

"So, when you headin' back to New Yoke?" asked Bunky, who sometimes had the habit of dropping his R's and always dropping them in New York.

This brother was straight-up country, and proud of it. Bunky was Dirty South before the South was the Dirty Dirty South. This southern boy had no plans to migrate to the northern Promised Land. Bunky, though, might have been on to something. Most of these folks, like my parents, found out the North fell short in keeping its promises. For many, it was not a respite from the open racism and discrimination of the South. What they found were ghettos filled with explorers like themselves, often segregated to the black belt of a community.

Daddy left Clayhatchee in 1949. Mama left in 1950. Story has it Daddy wanted to give his unborn children a chance for a better life; better schools, better opportunities, all the promises of the North to include those forty acres and a mule. After Daddy settled in Pittsburgh, he sent for Mama, who was already on her way. Daddy and Mama could count themselves among the millions of Black hopefuls in the nineteenth and twentieth centuries who looked toward the North Star for a brighter life. Like the immigrants from Europe, Black folks from the South settled into their own enclaves with like-kind, other Black Southerners who had done the same.

My parents lived in a newly minted housing project in Pittsburgh called the Lincoln Hill Apartments. The old folks liked to call it the Cracker Jack Box. I never knew why and never cared to ask. Nonetheless, newly arrived migrants from the South carrying years of discrimination, pain, and indignities packed into these city black belt districts, forming communities of love, laughter, and support. In this section of Pittsburgh, the Cracker Jack Box stood as tall as the Statue of Liberty, welcoming Black folks into their new existence. My father didn't have a difficult time, finding a job right away at the local mill, Lockman and Son Steel. He would stay there until he would be forced to retire forty years later as steel and steel cities such as Pittsburgh took a financial hit. L&SS, though, provided years of stability for John and Elaine, allowing them to raise a family and enjoy working middle-class status.

* * * *

"Hey, Bunky, do you know who Red Mansfield is?"
"Yeah, he was an old mean-ass white muthafucker. Why do you want to know about that dead-ass cracker?"
"He's not dead, Bunky."
"What do you mean he's not dead?"
"Just what I said. He's not dead. I saw him today at the funeral."
"Where? Lying in a coffin?"
"He's not dead. He was at Mama's funeral."
"Damn, if he's alive, he's older than Methuselah," Bunky said, cracking himself up. "But for real, he gotta be over a hundred years old. He was at your mama's funeral?"
"He was standing across the street."
"How do you know it was him? How do you even know about him?"
"I don't know anything about him. Some Black folks came out of the funeral home and said his name, and they seemed astonished to see him. Aunt Dee seemed to react to the man as well, but she didn't say anything. I just remember the crazy-ass look on his face."
"That was no look. That's his face. He's meaner than a rattlesnake. He hates Black folks. He scared the hell out of us kids when we were small. I thought he was a hundred years old then, Cuz. Red used to yell at us, calling us little niggers, pickaninnies, sambos, and any other degrading name his old decrepit ass could think of. Damn, I hated him. He had these German Shepherds. He would say he was going to sic his dogs on us. I can't believe he's still alive."
"Why would he want to come to Mama's funeral?" I asked.

"Ain't no telling. The old white bastard probably has Alzheimer's and thought he was going to a Klan rally. Yeah, it's kind of odd he would come out. No one has seen hide nor hair of him for at least fifteen or twenty years. I thought someone finally got tired of his white racist shit and did him in. He was still calling brothers "niggers" in 1986. And I'm not talking about young boys. I'm talking about people who would stab or shoot his redneck ass and wouldn't think anything about it. You know your daddy almost killed him."

"Really? How did he almost do that?"

"With a straight razor blade. Word is your daddy was pretty handy with a blade. Your daddy sliced off a piece of his left ear. Red used to have trouble hearing. I don't know if it was because of what your Daddy did or because he was just old. Nonetheless, he has less ear and a scar down the left side of his cheek thanks to J.R."

"So, why did my father try to kill him?"

"You know how bad niggas are and your daddy was a bad nigga. Just kidding, but he was bad. All I been told is Red owed your daddy something valuable, maybe money. I don't believe that shit. I do believe J.R. would have killed Red; that I don't doubt at all."

"You're right, Bunky. I believe Daddy would kill a man… if he was done wrong."

Bunky lit a Newport, the only way he could, pimp like. He shook the lighter a few times and flicked open the silver cover. Bunky hovered over the lighter and hunched his body as if it were twenty below and he was experiencing a harsh Chicago winter instead of a beautiful Clayhatchee summer. He tilted his head to the side as he lit the cigarette and then took a long purposeful drag, a French inhale, followed by smoke rings. Then he spoke.

"I always admired your daddy. He'd cut a cracker as quickly as he would a nigga. White skin didn't mean shit to him."

"All of this still doesn't explain why Red Mansfield decided he needed to be at Mama's funeral."

"You the big-time investigative reporter. Get your ass out and investigate. Come back with the story, Scoop," said Bunky, throwing his head back and roaring in laughter at his own hilarity.

I wasn't as amused. But, if I weren't in the middle of it, this would make a hell of a story. Heck, it still made a hell of a story. But I didn't have the time to chase ghosts, dig up the past, look for a paper trail. I was already working on a story and Lamont Bennett was the last piece of the puzzle before I could give birth to that sucker. I hadn't tried him in a couple of days because of the funeral, but I would have stopped damn near everything if Bennett had called. What time is it now? I should call him. It should be about 2 o'clock there. I wonder if he's at lunch. He's known for taking late lunches. Maybe I should wait until lunch is over. No, I'll call and leave another message.

I touched the number and waited. About the moment I thought the voice mail would kick in yet again, I heard a human.

"Hello," came from the receiver.

Damn, I can't believe I finally caught up with him.

"Hi, is this Lamont Bennett? This is James Kingsman, New York Daily. You are a hard man to reach, Mr. Bennett."

"Well, you got me now. What can I do for you?"

"I'm writing a story on housing and discrimination at your former workplace. What can you tell me?"

"Well, start asking questions; I'll see what I can tell you."

And with that opening, it was bombs away. I kept firing missiles. Some of them hit their mark, some missed the entire target. The ones that hit were dead on, bull's eye. I talked with Mr. Bennett for two hours, and after putting down the phone, I wrote furiously. I became a musician, a renowned pianist, pounding away for more than three hours. Oh, I was making sweet music on my laptop. It was pure joy. And I was done.

I looked over the arrangement of my story with modest satisfaction and e-mailed it to my editor. I had given birth again, and I was a happy man. It was finally done. As always, I was prepared for edits and comments and revisions and sarcasm. My hope was Cuddy wouldn't rip into it too much. I didn't want to get *Cuddied* by him. He was an old school editor in his late sixties—round, balding, loose tie, belly hanging over his belt, no nonsense. He had seen it all. Combat in Vietnam. In fact, Nam is where he began his journalism career as a public affairs officer. He covered the riots of 1968 after the assassination of Dr. Martin Luther King Jr. This white man was not scared to go in the darkest of neighborhoods if he thought there was a possibility for a story, especially if it was an above-the-fold front-page story.

No, Cuddy was as hard as they came, seldom tempered by political correctness or sensitivity. He demanded hard work and excellence and if a reporter or an assistant editor fell short, they were indeed *Cuddied*; a public berating and humiliation mixed with intimidation. Somehow, I had avoided being *Cuddied*, but I hadn't escaped Cuddy-free.

He didn't spare feelings much and told me on occasions that the baby (my story) was ugly (piss poor). I sure hoped this baby was a little cute. I couldn't believe how much and how vital the information was I gathered from Bennett. It was a provocative interview, and I wrote a story that hummed. Still, I figured Chief was going to give me grief over some aspect of the piece.

Quick with the slams and stingy with the compliments, Cuddy was still the best damn editor I knew. He was fair, he was honest, and he cared about his reporters, even if he didn't want to show it. He was a great teacher.

Again, I'd be on the road tomorrow and in the office two days later. By then, Chief will have twenty or so suggested changes. Oh, how I missed Cuddy, the job, Jackie… home.

I went to sleep thinking I would call Jackie as soon as I returned to New York. Sleep was sound and peaceful. And then Chuck D smacked me awake booming, "Elvis was a hero to most." As Public Enemy fought the power, I fumbled for my phone. With the ringtone silenced, the voice on the other end was grating, boisterous, and Cuddy's.

"Can you tell me, Kingsman, why in the hell am I getting work from you? Aren't you supposed to be at your mother's funeral?"

"Hey, Chief, how the hell are you?"

"Don't 'hey chief' me. Didn't we agree on a designated period for you to be off, so you could take care of your mother's affairs? Why do we plan if people aren't going to follow through? How are you doing, by the way, Kingsman?"

"I'm doing okay, Chief. Thanks for asking. Yes, we agreed on me being off, but I've been antsy. Once I got Bennett, the story practically wrote itself. And you've been waiting for it to be finished."

CARLISLE

"You're right, I've been waiting. And waiting another week wouldn't have mattered a bit. Anyway, I'm going to start running your piece on Sunday. It will run through Friday. You did a helluva job on it, Kingsman."

I tried to thank him, but Cuddy kept talking.

"You have one more week to yourself, Kingsman. If I see you in my newsroom any earlier, I might give you a pink slip. I don't want you here."

With that, he hung up.

"I'll see you in a week," I said.

I wondered what other enterprising stories were coming up? What story was the paper going to lead with today? Again, I missed the daily rhythm, the sounds, the deadlines. I must be nuts.

I was so fired up I couldn't sleep, so I decided to pack. I had my old Army duffel bag. Not classy, but it's how I like to travel, with old sturdy and reliable. I've been using the duffel bag since I was a kid, and through college. It was my dad's old Army bag. Hey, the green bag was home. As I put my black Gators in the bag upside down so the worn soles of the shoes were facing outward, Aunt Dee filled the doorway of my room.

"What you makin' all dat noise fo, James? I was gonna get my gun."

"I'm sorry Aunt Dee. I was just getting my things together so I can head out early in the morning."

"James, you don't have to leave so soon. You stay here long as you like. What's da rush?"

"Auntie, I have a lot of work back in New York. My editor needs to talk to me in person about this article I've been working on. I plan to leave at first daylight."

I have no idea why I was lying. It really hadn't been bad here. Actually, it had been nice seeing family and being around them—loving, laughing, remembering, learning. But it was time to move beyond my mother's death and mourning. Be firm. I'm out of here at daybreak, and not a minute later. There's nothing Aunt Dee could say that would keep me here. Nothing.

But she looked so sad. I had seen that look before.

"James, I've been wantin' to tell you sumpin since you arrived.

I didn't really know what to say or how to say it, but you a grown man now and you ready fo grown-folk talk. I think dis will help you understand some things."

Like the impolite reporters, particularly the prima donna types on television, I was more concerned about questions I had to ask rather than what Aunt Dee planned to tell me. I forged ahead.

"I'm sorry, Aunt Dee, before you tell me, I've had something on my mind I need to ask. May I?"

Aunt Dee nodded.

"What can you tell me about my daddy trying to kill Red Mansfield over money?"

"Who tole you dat?"

"I was talking to Bunky. He said he had heard that Red owed Daddy a bunch of money."

"Why you listen to Bunky and all of his foolish talk? Dat boy don't have da commonsense Gawd gave him."

"So, Daddy never tried to kill Red Mansfield?"

"I didn't say dat. But it wasn't ova no money. Dis is what I was tryin' to tell you."

"What are you trying to tell me, Auntie?"

"Yo daddy tried to kill Red Mansfield fo havin' his way wit yo mama."

My head pulsated, throbbed as if someone was priming it, trying to get my brain to start. I saw purple, red. My knees felt weak, and I needed to lean against something. Yes, the dresser would do. No, I needed to sit down.

"Are you saying Mama was raped by Red Mansfield?" I asked, incredulous I was posing this question to Aunt Dee.

"James, Red raped yo mama. She was fourteen. Red was probably in his thirties. He was strangely drawn to yo mama, always tryin' to talk to her. And I didn't do anything bout it until it was too late."

"What?" I looked up at Aunt Dee standing over me as I sat on the edge of the bed.

"Yo mama made me promise not to say nothin' to our daddy, and she especially didn't want yo daddy to know da comments Red made to her anytime he saw her. She knew your daddy woulda killed Red on da spot. I didn't say nothin', and I wish to dis day I had."

Aunt Dee wiped tears from her eyes, then continued.

"Red, wit help from two cracker friends, grabbed yo mama, who was walkin' home from school, and dragged her in a barn, and raped her."

"You uppity nigger. I tried to be nice, but you make it hard to be decent. No more. What or who you trying to save your monkey trim for, anyway? That good-for-nothing nigger, John, you so sweet on? Boys, I got it from here," Red said to Petey Smalls and Bakerfield Smith.

The girl tried to put up her arms to fight, but it just made Red angrier and his fists flew. Finally, Pudding rolled up in a ball and tried to cover her face and body from any more of Red's rage. Red pounced on top of Pudding; her schoolbooks scattered in his barn. With one hand holding her down, Red used the other hand to furiously grab at her dress. He pressed his hot tobacco breath on her face and neck. He then ripped her panties away, and as she started to scream, he forced himself inside, violently. She lay there crying. And she thought of John. And she cried some more. John, a proud boy, would not suffer this. And she thought of her father and mother and the shame of this moment.

And she thought about the pain and the white beast on top of her. And she prayed for rain to cleanse her. She prayed for thunder to silence her. She prayed for lightning to kill her. She prayed for death to gallop up on a white horse and smite them both.

I needed a moment. Disbelief and despair swirled around me. And as I was processing garbled thoughts, Aunt Dee said she had something else to tell me.

"I'll be right back," she said.

What else could she tell me? I felt like throwing up. I kept thinking of the puny snarling white man. Damn, he was at Mama's funeral. I wish I had this this information then. I wish I would have...

Then it came to me. I was going to finish what John Kingsman started. I was going to find the old bastard and kill him. Yes, this was the reason Mama asked me to bring her home. She knew I was the one strong enough to avenge her honor. It wouldn't take much doing to send Red to his grave. It was time to put the ghost to rest. I felt flushed and wet. My eyes burned as I wiped away salty tears.

As quickly as I had settled on killing Red, competing thoughts entered my mind. Forgiveness, First Baptist Church, Jesus, and Mama's voice all conspired to bring me back to reason. In a soft distance, I heard Mama reminding me vengeance is the Lord's. Didn't I remember this from all those years sitting in the pews of First Baptist? Red Mansfield was not worth throwing away my life. I wasn't a killer. But I did want to look the man in his eyes. I had to at least look the man in his eyes.

Aunt Dee returned with the photo album I had seen her looking through the other day. She sat on the bed next to me and began to flip through pages worn by time.

"Aunt Dee, you said Daddy tried to kill Red. What happened?"

She put the album down, making sure to keep her place. She put her hand up to her forehead, rubbing it a bit, and gave a large sigh

"Afta yo daddy learned of what Red did, he stormed outta da house lookin' fo him. Dey say yo daddy caught Red at Bottom Side. Yo daddy used a blade and sliced his face. He almost took off Red's ear. We thought yo daddy had kilt him. I guess Red was too ornery and mean to die. Dem white folks were gonna hang yo daddy. We got J.R. outta Clayhatchee fo da crackas had a chance to string him up."

"I always thought Daddy left Clayhatchee first to get things ready for Mama when she arrived. I didn't know he was running for his life."

"Well, yo daddy did prepare yo mama a place. Dat is da truth, but da truth also is he had to get outta town quick. Red had a large scar, and a vendetta against our family from dat day on. It was a happy time when Red disappeared cause da sight of him was always a reminda of all his ugliness."

"So, why do you think he was at the funeral? Do you think he was just trying to walk over Mama, walk over Mama in her grave, one last time, one more affront to our family?"

"As odd as it might seem, James, I don't think he was tryin' to disrespect yo mama. Red had some type of feelin's for Puddin', even if dey was twisted. He tried to make it up to Puddin' fo what he had done—buyin' her gifts, sendin' money. He was a devout racist who hated everything Black, except fo yo mama."

Aunt Dee looked away, then pointed to the photo album.

"Dere's one more thang," she said. "Yo mama became pregnant. She had a little girl."

Aunt Dee took me to the picture of a beautiful light-skinned baby with big green eyes and soft silky-looking hair. The baby couldn't be more than a few days old. The baby had Mama's eyes and nose. I couldn't see any of Red in her face. Good.

"So, what's the baby's name?"

"Well, she's no longer a baby. She's a grown woman now."

"Where is she?" I asked.

"I don't know."

"You don't know?"

"Chile, I *said* I don't know. Yo mama gave her up for adoption shortly afta she was born in 1950."

I had a sister out here and I didn't know where she was or even her name. Mama's lost daughter was the reason she couldn't keep Clayhatchee out of her mind. She had left a precious package here. That's why her heart could not be completely closed to Clayhatchee.

But Daddy couldn't stand Clayhatchee. Until the day he died, the place reminded him of his inability to protect his woman from being raped. Of all the South's indignities, this would have struck him to the core. If my father had stayed in Clayhatchee, he would have killed Red or died trying. No matter how many years had passed, he would still have murder in his heart and mind.

"Why didn't Mama tell Daddy about the baby?"

"Yo daddy wouldn't have been able to handle dat reminder in his face. Puddin' knew dat."

"Mama decided to leave her baby because of Daddy?"

"Yo mama didn't want him to know dat pain. She was ashamed. She was hurt. She didn't want yo daddy to live with dat shame."

"I am stunned..."

"J.R. left fo yo mama realized she was pregnant. He was on da run right afta he tried to kill Red. He was gone fo months fo he even contacted Elaine."

"So, she had already had the baby when he called for her?"

"Yes, truth be told, yo mama almost didn't leave Clayhatchee. She was torn. She didn't want to leave her baby but knew she couldn't take da chile wit her when she met yo daddy. She made da decision to give da baby up. It was done quick, and she was devastated. Her baby was gone. Da only relief she had was she could rid herself of Red forever and start her life with da man she loved. Elaine and J.R. could have dey own family without all da burdens of da past."

Elaine looked at her baby girl. Even as violence and hate swirled around the child's conception, Elaine could only feel love. The only trace of the baby's father was the color of her skin. Elaine, although fair-skinned, couldn't believe how pale her baby was. The baby's skin was so white Elaine's father couldn't even bring himself to look at her.

He wouldn't have to worry about that much longer. Elaine had decided to give her baby away. Ms. Ora Lee DeVough said a Black family from Atlanta had inquired about adopting a little girl. The father was a principal at the best Negro school in Atlanta and they already had two boys. They were a good family, pillars of the community. And with both of them being so fair-skinned, they wanted a light-skinned baby as well.

"It be time, Pudding," Ms. Ora Lee DeVough said as she came into the house with a new crib.

"Are you sure dey goin' to take care of my baby?"

"This family is one of the best Negro families in the South. Your child will not want for anything. She'll live like white folk. It be time, child."

Elaine instinctively stepped back as Ms. Ora Lee reached for the baby. Elaine pulled her baby closer to her chest. Her mind raced with her heart, and she was tired. She thought of how her father had detached himself from his white grandchild. She wondered if John would be able to love this child. She could not bear the idea he wouldn't, and she could not take that chance. And Red would hound her and the baby if they stayed. Elaine wanted to run with the child, but reality kept her immobile. Finally, her body and mind capitulated.

"You're doing right by this baby, Pudding."

Elaine turned her head as the little girl was pulled from her bosom. The demure baby let out a scream as Ms. Ora Lee DeVough gently put her into the crib.

"Pudding, you're doin' the right thing. This child is goin' to have a wonderful life. I promise you."

Elaine didn't say anything. She buried her head in her hands, stifling her screams.

Chapter 7
Stomping in My Timbs

My insides were churning. I was going to implode. I needed to leave the house. Take a walk. Do something. I needed to defuse. I needed a diversion. I needed to talk to Jackie. I needed to find that old white man. I wanted to look him in his face and ask him why he did it. Why would he dishonor my mama by coming to her funeral? I needed to confront him.

"Hey, Bunky, you said this is your town. I need your help."

"What do you need, Cuz?" Bunky asked on the other end of the phone.

"I need you to help me find Red Mansfield."

"So, you're still sure he ain't dead? Don't you have to get back to business in New Yoke?"

"No, he's not dead. And my business can wait for this."

"Cuz, you a wild dude. I don't know what you're up to, but I'm in. If Red is still among the living, we'll find him. I'll be over to get you, and we can take it to the streets. Them streets always know."

I hung up the phone with Bunky and, immediately, I thought I should call Jackie. I wasn't sure I wanted to burden her with old history and this new mess, but I wanted to talk to her. I missed my girl. And right now, with all that was going on, I needed to bounce some things off her. See if she could make any sense of it because I couldn't. As I started dialing Jackie, Aunt Dee walked back into the room. I hung up the phone.

"James, you okay? I know I told you more den you thought you wanted to know, more den I wanted to tell, but I thought it was time to bring it out."

My mind was elsewhere.

"Aunt Dee, do you know where Red Mansfield lives?"

"If da man I saw at da funeral was Red, you might be able to find him at da Herbert Lee Estate. But I don't think he has lived dere in twenty years. Until yesterday, everyone, including me, thought fo sure he was dead."

"Well, does he have any family members in the Herbert Lee Estate?"

"His wife died years ago, and his son and daughter left Clayhatchee a while back. Dey was a prominent family dat seemed to just disappear. So, what do you plan to do wit Red if you find him? What designs do you have, boy?" Aunt Dee lowered her head and put her hands on her wide hips, as she looked me in the eyes, daring me to give the wrong answer.

"No designs, Auntie. I just want to talk to him. That's all."

"Chile, don't be stupid. You have too much goin' on to worry bout some old white man, who if he ain't dead, has one foot in da grave. You have no time fo foolishness. Da time fo revenge is long gone."

"Who said anything about revenge?"

Aunt Dee gently touched my arm. She looked at me sorrowfully. "You don't have to say it, James. Yo eyes say everything. Doin' sumpin to dat man now is not gonna bring yo mama back. Leave it alone. It doesn't make any sense to conjure up old ghosts."

"I guess you're right," I said, pausing to think. "Aunt Dee, could I stay a few more days?"

"Chile, you can stay as long as you like," Aunt Dee said, hugging me tightly.

* * * *

I heard the front door open and close.

"Hey New Yoke, let's go!"

"Bunky," Aunt Dee yelled, "if you don't stop yellin' in my house…"

"Sorry, Mama. Is James upstairs?"

"He is."

"Can you tell him to shake a leg, that I'm here, Mama?"

"With all yo noise, I'm sure he already knows."

I leaped down the stairs and grabbed my Pittsburgh Steelers ball cap. Even though I lived in New York, I could never bring myself to wear any of their sports apparel. I would wear a Pirates jersey over a Yankees' any day and the Pirates were sorry... and they had been sorry for a long time. Even as I had looked forward to leaving Pittsburgh and a lot of its small-minded ways, I remained loyal to its sports teams. I was a diehard Steelers fan, looking toward the black and gold for the appropriate thug look today. I put on an old Greg Lloyd jersey; perhaps channeling some of the former linebacker's less than hospitable demeanor. I threw on some black jeans and my black Timberland boots. With my cap pulled down low on one side to nearly cover my right eye, my jersey tucked in the front to expose my large square gold buckle, my shirttail hanging out in the back and my Timbs laced to the top but not tied, I was feeling quite home-boyish, and it felt good. As I headed out into the southern streets of 2004 to find a 1940ish ghost, I needed to summon up some northern spirits of my own. Public Enemy, X-Klan, KRS1, Eric B &; Rakim—they would do. I needed all the help I could get to steady myself in my search for this man. I was apprehensive. I realized what my real concern was. It was me, not Mansfield. I wasn't concerned about what he would do. I worried about what I would do.

"Bunky, let's go," I said as I jumped down the steps, two, three at a time.

Chapter 8
Do a Little Dirt

"You ready to ride, Cuz?"
"I'm ready."
"I got a tip about where old Red Mansfield is hiding out. And you thought you were the only investigative reporter in the family."
"What? How did you find that out so soon?"
"You know that I can't reveal my sources. But the streets are hot. Are you ready to find this old cracker?"
"Yeah, let's go find the ghost. He has some explaining to do."
I put my hardest lean on, sinking into the car seat of Bunky's old Caddy, and went within as Bunky navigated the streets of Clayhatchee. Bunky stuck in his Anthony Hamilton CD, skipping through several tracks until he got to "Comin' From Where I'm From." *Sometimes you gotta do a little dirt.*

Anthony Hamilton takes you straight to the South with his lyrics. From Charlotte, North Carolina, the brother was straight up black-eyed peas and cornbread; a product of the new South. The Dirty South, as they called it. Bunky was part of this new South too. I wondered how different Bunky's upbringing in the former Confederacy was from my parents' life down here. Had the white man of the past been a boogeyman in the new South's present? Had Bunky's generation successfully killed the white boogeyman? Probably not. Most likely, the white boogeyman retired. His services were no longer needed. In the South, as it had been in the rest of the country, Black folks had often become their own worst nightmare—their own bogeymen. We killed each other without much thought over something as benign as stepping on someone's shoes, wanting someone's bomber jacket, dissing someone over drug money. Moreover, we weren't only doing each other bodily harm, we also had a role in destroying the spirit through heroin, cocaine, crack cocaine. Yeah, the South no longer needed a white boogeyman wearing white sheets to provide terror and destruction—Black folks had done a good job all by themselves.

Of course, that's just part of the story. The real boogeyman has always been the system. With its nearly four hundred years of brainwashing, oppression, and racism; the system had us out here losing our minds.

Sometimes you gotta cry a little bit louder. Preach! Anthony Hamilton. Preach on, brother.

Bunky and I hadn't said a word to each other for at least twenty minutes.

"Why are you looking for this old ass white man anyway?" Bunky asked, jarring the ride's silence.

"He raped my mother."

Bunky abruptly hit the brakes, causing the car to veer to the side of the road. The jolting stop made my head snap back.

"Did you say what I thought you said?"

"If you heard rape and my mother in the same sentence, then I said what you thought I said."

"Oh, hell no," Bunky said. "If he ain't dead, he will be. He better hope he's dead. If he's dead, he'll be one lucky dead muthafucker."

Bunky reached underneath his seat and grabbed his Glock. Bunky sat the gun between us on the seat, and he ranted. I didn't say anything. Bunky wasn't making much sense. He stopped making proclamations (thank goodness) and stared straight ahead. We sat in silence for a second time. Then, Bunky spoke.

"How do you know this? How did this happen?"

"I really don't want to get into this right now."

"OK. I feel you. So, Cuz."

"What?"

"What are you going to do?"

"I don't know."

"You don't know?" Bunky asked, both incredulous and indignant. "What's there not to know? This muthafucker raped Aunt Pudding. There's no time for indecision."

CARLISLE

Bunky's gangster took me by surprise. The brother was normally chill. This gangster posture was real, and Bunky now was asking me what I was going to do with all sincerity. And I didn't know what I was going to do. I had told Aunt Dee I only wanted to talk to the man, just to look him in the eyes. But that's not all I wanted to do. I wanted to pull his eyes out. I wanted to hurt him. I wanted to kill him. And now I was surprising myself.

"Let's find him first," I said.

"OK, I can do that."

We broke into silence again.

Yes, my mind was set. I came back to my initial thought. I would kill him. And I came back to that decision frighteningly easy, even before Bunky's incoherent rants. It was pretty simple. He raped my mother and he deserved to die. How many other Black women had he raped? How many other Black families had Red terrorized? I'm sure there was a litany of past sins that could be associated with this white bigot. But Red was not alone or the exception. Southern white rapists terrorized a countless number of Black women with impunity. Through the generations, countless Black men had to stand by emasculated, shamed, impotent, unable to perform the task of protecting their women, their daughters, their mothers. Well, not me. Not today. It didn't matter to me how deep in the past Red's crimes occurred. The fact they occurred was all that was important. I was deputizing myself. I was the sheriff coming into town, and why not? In the last twenty years, the U.S. Justice Department had reopened several criminal cases from the civil rights era of the 1950s and 1960s, hoping to get convictions before many of these old coots died. The feds had recently reopened the Emmett Till case, a boy of fourteen who was brutally killed for supposedly whistling at a white woman. About ten years earlier, the feds convicted Bryon De La Beckwith for killing NAACP field secretary Medgar Evers in his driveway in 1963. Beckwith was in his seventies when he was convicted. You can't run from your past forever. There's always a day of reckoning. Today was Red's.

Yes, I planned to let Red know who I was, see if he had something to say, and then I would put him down with Bunky's Glock. That easy.

That simple. Damn the consequences. Was I always this psycho? Had I always had a murderous heart? Had I been waiting for something to tap into this part of me? John Kingsman's name seemed to be written all over this new me. I had a sense of calmness to the idea of killing Red. His death wouldn't give back my mama's innocence, but it would be symbolic in destroying one of the last emblems of Clayhatchee's old South—white terror without retribution. Nope, killing Red wouldn't be too difficult.

I felt liberated, free as a bird, the wind blowing and the sun shining. But I didn't fly away. I was grounded and focused on the task.

"James, we're almost there, if my source is correct," Bunky said, proud of his journalistic vernacular. "Red's house should be the next street over."

Bunky turned onto a cobblestone road that led up a hill to a dead end. He pointed to the top of the hill, a house sitting in isolation, daring folks to disturb it. The home could have one time been a beautiful mansion, like in *Gone with the Wind*, but now suffered from years of neglect. The dilapidated house looked as if it were in a self-imposed exile. I was surprised. Hadn't he been rich? Why was he living like a pauper? It didn't matter, I guess.

"I think this is the house," Bunky said, looking more serious than I had ever seen. "You want me to go in with you?"

"Thanks, but this is something I need to do by myself."

"Well, here, take this," Bunky said as he pushed the Glock over to me. I grabbed it and put it in the back of my pants right at the small of my back. I had never been a gangsta, but I saw enough gangsta movies—*Boyz in the Hood, Juice, Menace to Society*—to know where to carry the piece and how to use it. I was ready for whatever.

Long chipped cement steps led to the ghost's home. As I marched up the stairs, I kept trying to think what I would say. Maybe I should just turn around. What was I doing? What was I going to do with this gun? Shoot him? Kill him? What would this look like—some big-time New York reporter killing an old local white recluse? Who was I kidding? But as I kept asking myself questions, I kept marching forward, visualizing our meeting. Red needed to answer for his crimes. One last step. Red needed to repent.

CARLISLE

I rang the doorbell. No one answered. I rang it again, and again, and again. No answer. I knocked on the door. No answer. I started pounding on the door. Nothing. I looked through the window. I couldn't see anyone. I turned around, headed for the steps, and resigned that I wouldn't meet the ghost today. Then, a boldness came over me. I decided to try the door handle. It opened. I went inside. Ready or not, here I come, ghost. My heart raced while my mind rested, steeped in full rationalization. That rationalization allowed my mind to slumber. And even as my mind slept, my body danced and chanted and advanced forward. My body came alive and was on fire. My body was leaderless as it prepared for war. I stepped inside the house.

The house looked bigger from the outside. Inside, it looked small and hollow—no furniture, no pictures, no warmth, no ghost. I became bolder. From the foyer, I moved from room to room. In the middle of the kitchen sat a small square table with one seat. Cereal and milk was abandoned on the table, a bowl of Captain Crunch half gone. The cabinet doors were open and bare but for a few scattered canned goods. Damn, the ghost was living badly. I decided to go upstairs. I had come this far. I needed to see if he was hovering, floating on the second floor. I wanted to see where the ghost went at night.

I grabbed on the railing that hung barely on its hinges and almost fell as it moved. At the top of the steps was the bathroom. A bucket with urine sat in the middle of the floor. There was a mud-stained towel hanging on the door. Disgusting.

I walked into the bedroom. It had dark blue drapes, a marble dresser, and a large bed. It was neat. It was clean. Nothing was out of place, except for the dead white man hanging from a rope tied off to a light fixture in the middle of the room.

The same white man I saw at the funeral had an expression of surprise on his face. Or was it a smirk? I stood and looked at the ghost, at Red Mansfield. This was the man who violated my mother. He didn't look like much. Frail, pale, naked from the waist up, and dead. He didn't look like much at all.

I walked closer to him. I had my gun out. He was dead, yet I still wanted to kill him. Yeah, I'll get that surprised smirk off his face. One bullet to the ghost's face should do it. As I fantasized squeezing the trigger, Bunky busted into the room.

"What did you do, Cuz? You hanged his old ass?" Bunky was wide-eyed, almost frightened.

"Naw, naw, naw. He was dead when I walked into the room. Someone got to him before I did."

"We need to bounce. Now," Bunky said with a sternness I didn't know was in him.

I started for the stairs, but Bunky didn't follow. I stopped a step away from the front door and turned. C'mon, Bunky! What was he doing? After about the longest sixty seconds of my life, he appeared at the top of the stairs. Like an old pro, he was wiping off everything he thought we might have touched. We ran out of the house, jumped into the car, and sped down the hill.

"You need to slow down. Don't give the police a reason to stop us," I said. "What took you so long?"

"I wanted to see if his dead ass had any money," laughed Bunky. "And he did, stashed in the dresser under some stinky underwear. I think there is at least a grand here."

Bunky started to hand me hundred-dollar bills. I pushed the bills away. I hadn't gone there to rob the man, just kill him. I might have been a would-be killer, but I wasn't a thief. Red Mansfield had been the thief. He had robbed from my grandfather, my father, and, most of all, my mother. I wasn't like him. I wasn't a thief at all.

"I don't want it, and you shouldn't have taken it. What if they trace that money back to us?"

Bunky stopped watching the road and turned to look at me.

"Why and how would anyone try to connect us to shorty's death? I'm sure there were a lot of people who wanted his ass dead and not all Black. Real talk."

With that, Bunky turned his head back to the road, seemingly unconcerned and a little annoyed by me.

"I wanted him dead. You wanted him dead," he continued. "We were going there to kill him, right? The money doesn't matter to him. He's dead."

It was good that Red was swinging in eternity, but I certainly didn't want to be fingered for his demise. And that made me a bit perturbed and worried about Bunky's heist.

"You shouldn't have taken the money," I said again.

"Well, New Yoke, what do you want me to do now? Should we turn around and take it back?" asked Bunky, not even trying to hide his irritation.

"No, it's too late. We need to figure some things out."

* * * *

Two days later, I still couldn't reach Jackie. I kept going into her voicemail. What was up with that? In addition, I had heard nothing about Red Mansfield. I hadn't seen Bunky since we left the ghost's house and wanted to get the hell out of Clayhatchee, but I had a strong need to know what would happen once somebody found the body.

I would stay another three days. If I didn't hear anything by then, I would leave without knowing. Hopefully, Bunky and I were in the clear. There's no way anyone would have known that we had been in Mansfield's house unless my cousin Bunky was flossing with that money. I wondered what Bunky was doing. I hope he wasn't flashing his money around town. He couldn't be that stupid.

Aunt Dee hadn't said much to me in the last few days. She was hospitable and warm as always, telling me I could stay there as long as I wanted to, that this was my home, but she was off somewhere in her own world and thoughts, and I was glad of that. I needed time with my own thoughts to make sense of all that had occurred. Even though Aunt Dee made sure I felt at home, I still felt like an interloper—not just in her home, but in the South. I needed to get back to the city, back to the North, back to Jackie.

"Hello."

"Jackie? Hey, baby, I finally got you."

"Hey, James. I'm sorry I missed your calls. My phone was acting up. All my calls were automatically going into voicemail. I'm still going through messages. Are you home?"

I barely heard her reason for not calling me back and it didn't matter. Her voice sounded like harps playing and I drank in the performance.

"No, I'm still in Clayhatchee. I'll be here for a few more days and then I'll head back."

"Why are you still there? I thought you would be back by now."

"I had to tie up some loose ends."

"Is everything all right, babe?" I loved it when she called me *babe*. She always said it with so much tenderness. Yes, I was her babe and she was mine. Maybe this meant we could patch up our relationship.

"Everything is cool," I lied. "How about you? Thank you again for going to Mama's funeral in Pittsburgh. I wish we…"

"James," she interrupted, "your mama was like a mother to me. I lost a mother too."

"Mama loved you like a daughter, Jackie, and I love you."

"I love you too, James."

"So, if we love each other, why aren't we together?"

"James, you know why."

"No, I don't. I told you nothing happened between me and that woman."

"Why did you have her number, James? Never mind, James. We're not having this conversation. There's no point."

"I love you."

"I love you too. I just don't trust you."

Ouch, I forgot how direct Jackie could be. I felt a bit wobbly. Damn, how do I repair a breach of trust? Jackie was resolute. Relationship or no relationship, I still needed my friend.

"Babe, I wish you didn't feel that way. It's just that…"

"What's going on, James?"

"I'm starting to uncover a lot of information about my family. It hasn't been all good. In fact, none of it has been good. It's one revelation after another. I'm ready to get home, and it would be good to see you regardless of our current relational status."

"James, you know where I live. You have my number. You can always talk to me. You know, you can always come to me. I'll be here when you get back to New York."

"I know. I hope we can work through this trust thing."

"We'll see about that when you make it back."

"OK, I'll see you in a couple of days."

CARLISLE

"See you then. Bye."

"Bye."

Not exactly what I had hoped for, but it was a start, maybe even a breakthrough. Yes, I'll try to make it right with Jackie when I get back. Jackie was family. If I didn't know that before, I knew it now, and there's something to be said about family. Until this trip, I hadn't really thought much about the importance of family. Except for the way I thought about my parents, I had viewed family narrowly—a burden, people to deal with, to endure, siblings to fight with. Aunt Dee and, strangely enough, Bunky were helping me to reevaluate. Having a family of my own was still a major leap, but if I were going to make that leap, it would be with Jackie, no doubt. Why in the world did I take that woman's number and why was I so stupid to keep it?

Aunt Dee walked into my room with the *Clayhatchee Daily* in her hand. She dropped the newspaper on my bed. On the front page, the headline screamed "Prominent Citizen Murdered in Bedroom." The story ran above the fold with the byline Mark Taddy. I always made a point to never skip the byline. The writer should get his or her recognition.

Before I could jump into the story, I was stopped by the picture. Staring at me was the ghost when he was younger, maybe in his mid-thirties. It was a black and white photo. He had a part down the middle of his head and wasn't a half-bad looking guy. I wondered how the paper came upon this photo if he didn't have any family around.

Aunt Dee waited for me to finish the story. She didn't say anything as I read. When I looked up, she had a wide-eyed look on her face. It was a bit surprising. It's one of those looks not associated with an old woman, but a young one who has been dogged out so many times by her man that she doesn't know which way is up. It was a strange look coming from Aunt Dee.

"You see, James, when people do evil, it has a way of catchin' up wit dem," my aunt said as she turned and left the room.

It sure enough had a way of catching up with the ghost. He had it coming. Lord knows he had it coming. I wondered who gave it to him.

Chapter 9
Brother Man Down

My sleep had been restless. And that wasn't good because I needed my rest. I was ready to leave family, ghost, and old history here in Clayhatchee. I had only been here for nearly a week, and it seemed as if it had been a lifetime. I'm with you Dad; they can have Clayhatchee. It was time to get home.

I grabbed my duffel bag from the closet once again, tossed it on the bed, and started packing my clothes from the two top drawers that Aunt Dee gave me. I didn't bring a lot of clothes. My focus had always been to just take care of Mama's request and return home as quickly as possible. But, as I was throwing my jeans in my bag, I heard a blood curdling scream from downstairs. I ran down to find Aunt Dee passed out on her couch as Aunt Earlene rushed to her. All hell had broken loose.

The police arrested Bunky for the murder of Red Mansfield. The police found Bunky's prints on the ghost's dresser, ran a check, and it came up Walter Macklin, aka Bunky, who had experienced some minor scrapes with the law, mostly for drug peddling. The prints weren't all the police discovered. They found the money on Bunky's dumb ass. I told him to leave the money. Bunky had just personally closed the cell door on his Black ass. I needed to get the hell out of Clayhatchee, but I couldn't leave now. I was in the thick of it.

Aunt Earlene was fanning Aunt Dee, who had come to and was sobbing unbearably and muttering, "My baby, my baby," between sobs. During the day, other family members and friends sojourned to Aunt Dee's house to commiserate and comfort her. All of Bunky's family were at the house. His wife, Gloria, wept hysterically in the corner chair, holding her child ReCe.

CARLISLE

Gloria had also brought Bunky's two biological children that he'd had with Lori, Nikki, a girl of about thirteen, and his eight-year-old son, Walter Macklin Jr., to the house. Little Mack—that's what they called him—busied himself with a game board, oblivious to the fuss going on around him. Bunky's oldest child, Nikki, matched Aunt Dee in her hysteria, clinging to her mother's side. I half expected Bunky's girlfriend Wanda and Little Man to appear. They certainly would not have been out of place. Family, neighbors, friends were going in and out of the house. The phone rang off the hook. Chaos.

Cousin Willie grabbed me and said we should go and check on Bunky's arraignment and see if he would make bail. I knew it was unlikely that bail would be set and, if by chance it had, unlikely Bunky or anyone else in the family would have the money to post it. You had a capital case, a Black drug dealer (albeit petty), a prominent old white dead man, and stolen money. It wasn't looking good for Bunky. Not to sound self-absorbed, but I did wonder if Bunky had mentioned my name. No, he wouldn't. If he had, the police would have come and hauled me off as well. A northern Negro. Yeah, I'm sure he hadn't said anything. And I didn't think he would. But I wasn't going to worry about that. I was going to find a way to get my cousin out of jail for something he didn't do. This was not his mess. Yes, he took the money, but he wouldn't have even been in the ghost's house if it hadn't been for me. Bunky had my back. I needed to have his.

Chapter 10
Stay Strong

Bail denied. Not a surprise. Nonetheless, Bunky's public defender could have put up a little fight; at least give the appearance your client is innocent, and you believe in his innocence. It's no wonder so many Black men find themselves locked up in a system that stacks the deck against them from the beginning, particularly if they're Black and poor. Your ass is poor, so you have to accept some weak attorney. Now that same public defender is the one out front trying to convince a jury of not your peers that you're innocent. The first thing we had to do is find Bunky a real lawyer, a brother; a Johnnie Cochran-type. I couldn't let my cousin go down for something he didn't do because he had some marginal public defender. We would find some money to get him a good lawyer, and I would make it my business to find out who killed Red Mansfield. I went from chasing the ghost to now chasing a shadow, a deadly shadow.

    I sat in the waiting room with Willie and Aunt Dee in the county jail. All county jails look the same no matter the county, city, or state. I hated visiting jails, but it seemed difficult to avoid. There was always a steady stream of people I knew who were either going in or being released. And when a family member or friend found himself or herself on the wrong side of the law, there was an obligation to go visit that person, knowing the gesture would be reciprocated when you did your bid in the county. I had visited too many of my homeboys and family members in jail, and those trips in my young adult life made me determine early there would never be a need for anyone to reciprocate my gesture. No, I wouldn't need any of them to tell me to keep my head up and to stay strong as we talked between a plated glass. No way. I hated jails, hated seeing Black people in them.

CARLISLE

I hated seeing people I love locked up like animals in those bright orange jumpsuits.

When we arrived, we were searched. The guards even searched poor Aunt Dee, who didn't flinch. We waited in a nondescript sixteen-by-twenty room with gray walls with at least twelve other Black folks commiserating about their incarcerated loved ones. I saw a lot of mothers. There were always mothers dragging along their children to see daddies who were doing yet another stint in the joint.

One little girl with pigtails, couldn't be older than five, refused to listen to her mother, or was it her grandmother? I couldn't tell because the woman appeared to be in her forties, with a touch of gray. She was dressed modestly in a blue pants suit. The woman admonished the little girl who kept standing on her seat. While the little girl was standing on her seat, she also was begging the woman for gum out of the candy machine. When the woman told her no, the girl began to scream at the top of her lungs. The woman didn't even yell at the little girl to be quiet. The dark-skinned woman pulled a belt from her purse and started swinging it with precision. OK, she was the grandmother. Mothers would have been still either yelling or trying to talk to the child, but not an old school grandmother. This woman told her grandchild if she didn't stop making all that noise, she was going to beat the Black off her; which I always found a curious statement. How do you beat the Black off someone, and more importantly, why would you want to? I guess the girl didn't want to find out. She stopped crying. Grandmother stopped beating, and the five-year-old sat her behind down.

The guard began to yell out names—"Benson, Brock, Jefferson, Ford, Jones..." It was time for the second wave of visitors. When we arrived at 11:30 a.m., we had missed making the list for the first group, which meant we had to wait an additional hour before we could see Bunky. Finally, the guard led us in for the thirty-minute visit, and we filed into the room that separated us from the prisoners by a glass wall. The prisoners then filed into the room. I saw my cousin coming into the room, outfitted with his very own county orange jumpsuit. My gosh, those suits are ugly. It couldn't be bad enough you were incarcerated, but you also had to sport that bright glow-in-the-dark jumpsuit. We were assigned booth eight, which was only big enough for one person, although Aunt Dee, Cousin Willie, and I were all trying to squeeze into the box. Aunt Dee talked to her son first. I was surprised no phone was needed to talk. Aunt Dee and Bunky reached for each other touching the glass with their fingertips before they started speaking. Bunky gave a head nod to Willie and me. Aunt Dee wiped away a tear.

"You alright, baby?" she asked, voice quivering, unsteady and unsure.

"I'm fine, Mama. I appreciate that you're here, but you don't need to be in this place. I wouldn't be here if I didn't have to be. How are Gloria and the children?"

"Dey at my house. Gloria didn't want to bring da children here, and she didn't want to leave dem alone right now. She said she be down to see you next week," Aunt Dee said, refusing to drop her stare.

"Are they doing okay?" Bunky asked Aunt Dee, who was still staring.

"Dey as good as can be expected in dis situation."

"Has anyone talked to Lori? How's Little Mack and Nikki doing?"

"Little Mack acts as if he couldn't care less and Nikki is blubbering all over da place. Those are yo kids; you know how dey are. Lori is takin' care of dem. She's a good mama. Are dey treatin' you okay in here?"

"They are treating me fine. You know Skeet is in here. I saw Bubba too. All of my old friends are in here. Nothing for you to worry about, Mama. I should be just fine."

"Skeet n Bubba hur?" Willie asked. "How dey doin'? How dey mama doin'? Lawd, dey mama's fine. Whad dey do?"

"You know, the usual—drugs. You know they both sold to the same undercover police officer. Do you believe that?"

"Dem boys aine neva bun smart," Willie said laughing.

Aunt Dee wasn't amused. And I didn't know who they were talking about, but it didn't matter. I knew those brothers just the same. Drugs, the ghetto, Black men, and jail.

"You need to stay clear of dem boys," Aunt Dee said. "Since dey was little dey been up to no good. Doze boys will get you in trouble. You hear me, Bunky? Doze boys ain't nothin' but trouble."

CARLISLE

"Mama, I'm already in trouble. I'm already in big trouble."

For the first time, Aunt Dee looked away from Bunky. And still looking away, she asked Bunky what had been on her mind.

"Did you kill old Red Mansfield?" she asked, not giving him time to answer. "If you had, I wouldn't blame you. He had it coming for a long time, and the world is sure enough a better place without him. But his life isn't worth yo life, son. His life is nowhere near the worth of yo life. I know you didn't kill dat man. Dat would be a fool thang to do, and I didn't raise a fool."

Bunky started to chuckle and shaking his head.

"Mama, you know they record this conversation and that's the type of question my lawyer wouldn't want me answering. Your son is no fool. I don't know how the man ended up dead, but it wasn't by me. That's for damn sure. Sorry for cussing, Mama."

"Well, Bunky how you gonna explain how yo prints all ova his house? Ain't dey your prints dey found all through the house? What were you doin' at all in Red's house? What were you doing with all dat money?"

Damn, this was the longest thirty minutes of my life. I wanted to tell Aunt Dee her boy was innocent. I was with Bunky. I was with Bunky up to my neck in this mess. I had murder in my heart, but I didn't kill anyone, nor did Bunky. It was a cursing and a blessing that someone did Red Mansfield before we got there. Who knows what I would have done. I'm glad I'll never have to find out. But the mere fact I went to his house could implicate me in his death. Bunky already had been implicated, and he was feeling the heat. I felt it would be just a matter of time before someone started asking about the Yankee stranger. I couldn't even tell Aunt Dee how I knew her boy was innocent.

"There's nothing to tell, Mama. I didn't do it."

The guard came by letting us know we had five minutes left. Aunt Dee said she was ready to go. Her boy said he didn't kill Mansfield, and that was good enough for her. I asked Willie if he could take Aunt Dee to the car. I needed to talk to Bunky. Aunt Dee put her hand up to the glass.

"Son, I'm goin' to pray fo you. I'm goin' to pray dat justice be done. Da good Lawd ain't gonna let you sit in dis jail for sumpin you ain't done. You won't be in here long. Justice will be served."

Willie held Aunt Dee by the arm as the elderly woman shuffled out of the room. On his way, Willie pounded his chest over his heart and then pointed to Bunky with a peace sign. Bunky did the same. It was the "I got your back, stay strong, hold your head up brother" universal Black sign. And what other choice did a brother have in this situation but to stay strong? With them out of the door, I moved closer to the glass.

"So, how are you really doing?"

"I'm ready to get the hell out of here, Cuz. They are trying to pin it on me. And *you* know I didn't do it."

"What are they saying? What have they asked you... what have you told them?"

Bunky leaned toward the glass.

"Nothing."

I knew what he meant. And I didn't need to ask him any more questions along those lines.

"Listen, Cuz," he said. "I'm not going to be able to make it with this public defender. This fool is already telling me I need to plea. He says the DA has an open-and-shut case. He had the nerve to say it would be in my best interest to plea guilty. Can you believe that?"

"Alright, man, I'm going to get you a lawyer. You're going to get out of this. I'm going to find you a good lawyer."

"Johnnie Cochran-like?"

"Better than Johnnie Cochran. And don't worry about money. I'll go check on your girlfriend and wife to see what they might need."

"I appreciate your help, Cuz. I won't forget it."

"It's the least I can do."

"Time's up," yelled the beefy guard, who looked like a white version of the magical Black inmate in the *Green Mile* movie.

"I'll keep in contact." With nothing else to say, I told Bunky to stay strong.

When I reached the car, Willie and Aunt Dee looked like they were more than ready to be gone. I apologized for holding them up.

"So, what you and my boy need to talk bout in private?" Aunt Dee asked.

CARLISLE

"I just wanted to make sure he was okay and to let him know we were going to find him a lawyer."

"Dat's all?" Aunt Dee asked as she looked me up and down.

"That's all, Auntie. He's doing as well as can be expected, but he needs a new lawyer. This public defender is going to get him life. I have a lot of lawyer friends, but we need to find someone who's already here. Also, we need to find him a good lawyer. Do you know anyone?"

Willie stroked his beard with his right hand as he kept his left hand on the wheel. He was no longer concentrating on the road, but on my question. Aunt Dee was in her own feelings and thoughts.

"When de Black folks git in trouble, dey call Geckman," Willie said, breaking the silence. "Jewiss lawya. Yeah, Geckman de man."

"There aren't any Johnnie Cochrans down here?" I asked. "You don't know of any Black lawyers?" I wasn't trying to be racist or closed-minded. I just thought a Black man might be more invested in keeping another Black man out of prison.

"Nah, Geckman de man," Willie again emphasized.

"I don't care what color of a lawyer you get. I just want my baby home," Aunt Dee said, as she started to tear up.

"Willie, get me the number to Geckman."

Chapter 11
Pudding

Every time I used Aunt Dee's phone, I cracked up. She probably had the last rotary phone in Clayhatchee. I didn't think they made these phones anymore. I normally would have used my cell phone, but with all the commotion, I forgot to charge it. I needed to talk to Cuddy about the time off he offered. I probably needed it before this mess, but I was being stubborn.

I have this thing about being irreplaceable at the job, or at least, thinking I'm irreplaceable. I always believed I needed to do more, sacrifice more, work the weekends and holidays and graveyard shifts, don't take vacations or sick days, scoop the competitors and my colleagues—just work and scoop. This work ethic had proven beneficial to my career.

After only being at *The New York Daily* for two years, I was awarded a coveted city hall beat. After four years there, I was named a special projects reporter, which provided me with the freedom to pursue the types of long-term stories I wanted to do and felt were important. I had worked my butt off and I had the respect of my editors and colleagues. But as a reporter, you're only as good as your last story. That's truer as a Black reporter at a major newspaper. I couldn't afford any slips—white reporters could, Black reporters couldn't. Work. Nonstop.

"Hey, Chief, this is James. How's it going?"

"It's going well here. More importantly, how are you doing and when are you coming back?"

"Well, Chief, that's why I'm calling. I'm going to need the time you offered me earlier. One of my family members is in trouble, and he needs my help."

"You want to take time off? It must be bad. What's going on?"

CARLISLE

"It's really bad. Murder. He's been accused of killing an elderly white man from Clayhatchee. Right now, I am trying to find him a lawyer. He didn't do it, and his lawyer, a public defender, is trying to get him to plea out to second-degree murder. Well, I can't let him go to jail for life for something I know he didn't do."

"James, no disrespect, but how are you so certain he didn't do it?"

"I can't go into the details, but I am absolutely certain he's innocent. Trust me."

Cuddy didn't say anything, just a long pause and the sound of heavy deliberate breathing. There weren't many things that would put Cuddy at a loss for words.

"James, are you in any trouble?"

"No, I'm not in anything. But I need to stay here longer. I'm not sure how much time it will take."

"OK, take some more time, but you need to stay in touch with me. I need to know what's going on."

"Thanks, Chief. I really appreciate this."

"James, take care of yourself. And I'll be hearing from you soon."

"All right, Chief. Talk to you soon."

OK, at least that went well. Not too many things had gone well since I returned to Clayhatchee. I hadn't seen the beauty of this place Mama had talked about so often. What was I missing?

> "She's the most beautiful baby I've ever seen," Victoria said to Ora Lee DeVough.
>
> Five days earlier, Victoria had miscarried in silence. Red had thought his wife's trip to a midwife was a false alarm, but Ora Lee had told her not to fret. There was a brand new baby girl whose mama was unable to take care of her. The mother was a light-skinned Black woman who had been in relations with a white man, but no one would ever suspect this baby had Negro blood in her veins. Victoria didn't hesitate. She would pretend she was still pregnant and bring the baby home as hers. A few days later, Victoria was staring at her new white baby.

"I think we'll name her Katherine Lee Mansfield. Are you sure she's not going to get any darker?"
"Miss Victoria, this baby's mother is darn near white. This is about as dark as she gonna get. This baby is your baby. Rejoice, Ma'am."
Victoria took in the child fully with her eyes and heart. She kissed the baby on her cheek and young Katherine cooed.
"Miss Victoria," said Ora Lee, "the baby's birth mama needs a little money to get her on her feet. She'll be much obliged with a generous offer from you."
"Who is this child's birth mother?"
"Miss Victoria, that's not that important. You don't need to know those little details."
"I do need to know if I'm going to be handing her money."
"This baby here was birthed by Elaine Williamson. They call the girl Pudding."
"I know that sweet child. Who is the pappy?"
"I truly don't know. Can I get some money to help the girl get out of Clayhatchee?"
"Certainly," Victoria said. "You don't know what this child will mean to my family. Send someone to fetch Red. He needs to know he's a pappy again."
A week later, in the mail, Elaine received a bus ticket to Pittsburgh and $300. She never sought out the donor. She was leaving for a new life with John.

I reached Geckman. He would take the case and meet with Bunky this week. That was good. I couldn't sit still. I needed to do some investigating for myself. Yes, if there was a time that I needed to use my journalism skills, this was it. What happened to the ghost? I needed to ask questions without drawing any attention to myself. I could write an in-depth story about Red and his mysterious death. That should provide enough cover for me. Hell, I could contact Cuddy and see if *The New York Daily* might be interested in this story. Looking at this purely in a journalistic sense (and forgetting for a moment that my family was involved, that I was involved), this was a great story. Yeah, I needed to talk to Chief about this.

"You want to do what?" Cuddy said not trying to hold his disbelief.

"I want to write a story about Red Mansfield's death and the arrest of my cousin for the paper."

"The ethical and legal issues are numerous. Have you gone mad from the southern heat?"

"No, I'm still sane, for now. Look, Chief, I know there might be some ethical considerations, but I would not compromise objectivity and would be in favor of full disclosure in the publication. I think this is a legitimate story. It has everything—murder, race, money, old South, new South, a young Black man accused of killing a prominent white racist. Plus, from what I can tell this Red was a notorious racist who, along with his KKK brothers, probably has some blood on his hands. In addition, I hear his family is filthy rich. There might be an inheritance involved. His last years were spent as a recluse. He lived like a pauper. He has two living children. I'll start with them to find out who this guy was from their perspectives. When the other national newspapers hear this story, they'll be here. We have a jump on them. I'm already here at no cost to the paper."

"OK, you're back on the clock. I want stories weekly. You understand?"

"Chief, you're not going to ease me back into work slowly," I asked, half-jokingly.

"Nope. You did a heck of a job selling me on this story. My job is to sell newspapers. I'll expect to see a story by deadline on Wednesday. Don't miss deadline. Oh, one more thing. Don't get yourself killed or jailed. I got to go."

Okay, there was no question about it. I was officially back to work. And it felt good even in the middle of this mess. Work always energized me. And, yes, I understood the ethical issues of being an inherent conflict of interest, but I didn't care. The fact that Bunky was innocent only motivated me more to get it right.

Chapter 12
The Ghost Killer

Who would want to kill the ghost? Who wouldn't want to kill him? Red Mansfield did a lot of dirt through the years. But that was years ago. Most of the Black folks he antagonized were dead or too old to remember, too old to care. For those my age, he was the boogeyman—a reminder of the past when Blacks lowered their eyes in the presence of white people. I needed to talk to someone who knew the ghost when he was flesh and blood and all hell. But first I needed some background information. It was time to do some reporting.

I started by going to Clayhatchee's county clerk and found out that Red Mansfield had numerous run-ins with the law—public drunkenness, lewd behavior, assault. Red was a rich man, but he lived and acted like poor white trash. Most of his acts involved Black women, although he was arrested in 1946 for attacking Delores Tibit, a white woman. Tibit might as well have been Black; white trash as many folks would have called her then. She was easy prey for Mansfield, who never seemed to get into any real trouble with the law. Quite possibly, his money and connections were getting him out of a lot of scrapes, even with a white woman.

I followed with a trip to the library so I could log onto the internet to find out more information on Mansfield. Many of his arrests were reported in the local newspaper, but generic such as this one dated Oct. 6, 1944— "Red Mansfield arrested for misconduct involving a colored girl." In fact, the only time, Red was in any danger of going to jail was when he was arrested and set to go on trial for the Tibit attack. It didn't take long, however, for the jury to exonerate Red. In the newspaper clipping, dated May 1, 1946, there was a picture of a smiling Red coming out of the courthouse.

There was another picture of Red Mansfield smiling as well, just six months later. He was coming out of a church with his new bride, the socialite Victoria LeBeuth. Her daddy had owned Stockdale Insurance Company.

When I had asked Aunt Dee about Red Mansfield's wife, she answered, "Miss Victoria... now, dat was a good woman. Gawd bless her soul."

I wondered why the LeBeuths would give their only daughter, the cream of southern white womanhood, to the likes of Red Mansfield. Of all the eligible men, they chose a serial rapist, or at the very least, a serial abuser of women, for their daughter to share a bed with for the rest of her life.

There was more to the story.

After some more digging, I found that Victoria's father—Theodore LeBeuth—had been a successful businessman whose family had left the slave and cotton business. The LeBeuths built a fortune with investments. However, when the stock market crashed in 1929, the family's fortune went with it. Although Theodore pulled his family from the ashes of the Great Depression, his wealth was never the same. Even so, the LeBeuths still carried the respect of a good name—based on old laurels, good deeds, and prestige. The Mansfield upstarts coveted the LeBeuth name and the LeBeuths needed capital. It appeared to have started as a marriage of convenience.

It also appeared Red stayed out of trouble (or at least out of the papers) for the most part after he married Victoria. Later clips announced the births of their children, Robert on June 23, 1947 and Katherine May 14, 1950. I wondered where those two were. I needed to find them. Would they appear at the trial? Would they be home for Mansfield's funeral? When was the funeral? I hadn't seen an announcement. Finding information on Mansfield's funeral was top priority.

An old newspaper clip showed that Victoria Mansfield died nearly thirty-five years ago. According to the article, there had been a huge gathering at her funeral. Victoria was praised for her philanthropic activities in Clayhatchee. In the photographs, Black and white people alike were frozen in time grieving for Mrs. Mansfield. It was funny;

Red was not in any of the pictures. In one photo, young Robert and Katherine were pictured looking on as their mother was being remembered. I couldn't help but notice how strikingly different brother and sister were. Robert was a small man with soft features. He looked a lot like his mother, whereas, Katherine was tall strikingly beautiful.

I found a funeral announcement for Red Mansfield. Bad news—it was closed to the public and occurred two days ago. The announcement named Katherine and Robert E. Mansfield as his only living relatives. I couldn't find much more on Red, even during the civil rights turmoil of the 1950s and 1960s. It doesn't mean he wasn't still doing dirt. In fact, Aunt Dee had told me earlier that Red and some of his redneck friends killed Charles Jackson, a Black man who had made a pass at Katherine in the summer of 1967. Jackson had been found hanging from a tree with his genitals removed. Aunt Dee said, as sure she was Black, she was certain that Red had something to do with the murder.

"Aunt Dee, who do you think would have wanted to kill Red?"

"Lot of folks had a reason to kill dat old devil. Black folks ain't cryin' cause he's dead."

"Do you think any white folks here could have wanted to see him dead? Had he done any white folks wrong? How about the Tibits? Didn't he assault that Tibit girl?"

"How you know bout dat?"

"I've been doing my homework."

Aunt Dee cocked her head to the side, the way she always did when she was thinking, and stared up at the ceiling before answering.

"Yes, da Tibet family would probably still want retribution. I thought dat rapist was finally gonna go to jail. He had messed wit a white woman dis time, but da lack of justice she received made her as Black as any colored girl in Clayhatchee. Delores's daddy was a drunk, and her mama was known fo bein' loose. No one ever took Delores's claims seriously, especially not da jury. Didn't take dat long fo da jury to come back with a 'not guilty' verdict. It was da talk of da town. Ain't no justice fo po white trash girls."

"Do you know if she is still around the area?"

"She left home right afta da trial. People say she couldn't stand being thought of as havin' whorish ways, and dat's how Red's lawya portrayed dat po girl. Just ruined da little bit of reputation she had. The parents stayed in seclusion and died a few years back. She had two younger brothas, but no tellin' where dey are now, if dey even alive. Again, how do you know bout Delores Tibit?"

"I've been doing a little research at the library, Auntie. What more can you tell me about Charles Jackson's family? Does he still have any family here?"

"If you so good at research, boy, why didn't you find out dat his mama lives in Clayhatchee on Trafford Hill? She been dere for years. Ruby Jackson. You should be able to find her in da phone book. She lives alone. Charles Jackson Sr. died shortly afta junior got hanged. People said Senior died of a broken heart. Ruby was always stronger den her husband. Yes, Ms. Ruby would talk to you. She a good woman, a Gawd-fearin' woman. You got to have faith to deal wit what she has had to endure. Da good Lawd knows. I gots to have faith now too; faith dat I'm not goin' to lose my boy like she lost hers."

Aunt Dee stood up from her chair and slowly made her way out of the room.

"You're not going to lose Bunky, Auntie. I promise you that."

Why did I push her? I needed to be more sensitive. She wasn't just any old source I was interviewing for a story, she was family. This wasn't some story that didn't have any impact on my life. This was about my cousin in a jam that I put him in. Maybe Ms. Ruby would have an idea who might have murdered Red.

Finding her was easy, the only Ruby Jackson in the phone book. More importantly, she was lucid for an elderly woman and eager to talk to me. Her son had been murdered thirty-seven years ago, but she still had not given up the notion that justice would come to her boy's killer. She told me to come by today.

Ms. Ruby lived in the historical section of town known as Sugar Hill. Since the early 1900s, Sugar Hill housed the refined of the community—the Negro middle class, the bourgeois. It played home to teachers, doctors, preachers, funeral home directors, and others who had accumulated Black wealth and status. Desired because of its location and historical significance, Sugar Hill saw developers come in, remake, and change its very essence. New development that catered to high income, mostly white people ushered in Clayhatchee's internal migration. Many Black families left the Hill, as they affectionately like to call it, under the weight of construction and integration and gentrification.

Ruby Jackson didn't leave. After her son's death, the national press—Black and white—wrote extensively about the hanging. The reporting brought pressure locally for an arrest. The Willowbrook boys, Roy and Jack, were hauled in for the murder. The Jackson's wealth and good name was respected by both races. The Willowbrook's paucity and bad name, viewed as rednecks, led to their conviction. It was a rare moment—white boys found guilty in the death of a Black boy. In addition, their public defender didn't do the boys any help, probably causing them more years in the state penitentiary.

However, many of the town's folks, including the Jacksons, never believed the Willowbrook boys were solely responsible for Charles's death. Yes, it was a victory for civil rights, but it was the wrong white men. People whispered Red Mansfield's name.

"Until the day I die, I'm not going to stop believing that cracker killed my beautiful boy. Red Mansfield finally got what he deserves, and I hope he's burning in hell," said Ms. Ruby, a tiny fair-skinned woman, looking squarely at me with scrunched eyebrows. She had a head full of white hair, which was braided down her back. Ms. Ruby, still a beautiful woman, undoubtedly turned more than a few heads in her day. She was a spry woman, who could have easily been in her sixties rather than nearing ninety. She moved with ease, and there was fire in her eyes; green eyes that hid behind wire-rimmed glasses that set squarely on a petite narrowed nose. Ms. Ruby had been a teacher in the colored schools, her husband a principal.

"So, the Kingsman are your kinfolk?" she asked.

"Yes, Ma'am."

"I am sure I have taught many of your relatives, young man. As memory serves me, most of them were good students. Didn't give me much trouble. So, you're going to write a story about how Red Mansfield killed my boy?"

"Ma'am, I'm actually writing a story about Red Mansfield's murder.

CARLISLE

I'm trying to find out who would want to kill him."

"Red was a despicable man, who finally got his due," Ms. Ruby said, her voice steady as she talked about the ghost. "Red had my boy killed. I know it as sure as I am standing here and the rest of the people in town know it. I don't know why they hauled those Willowbrook boys off to trial. Red told my boy he was going to get him."

Ms. Ruby paused a minute, looked up, and shook her head.

"Lord knows I shouldn't hate this man, this close and all to being called to Heaven. I've prayed about it for years, and maybe with his death, God will open my heart, but I been carrying this for so long, young man. I'm tired."

"I can understand that, Ms. Ruby. Ma'am, could you tell me why you think Red killed Charles?"

"He wanted Charles dead because his fast little daughter was sweet on my boy. How couldn't she like him? Charles Jr. was beautiful. He had good hair, his skin was light, almost white, and he was smart. Charles came from good stock. That girl couldn't help but like Charles, colored or not. Red caught his fast-tail daughter kissing my son. Then he took it out on my boy."

Ms. Ruby reached for a tissue. She looked small.

"Ms. Ruby, I didn't mean to upset you. We can stop if you want to."

"Why would I want to stop, young man?" she said, looking up at me. "Don't worry about a sentimental old woman. You have some questions. I'll try to answer them for you."

"OK. Why wasn't Red Mansfield arrested?"

"Money. Red owned this town, and he owned the law in it. In addition, he set those Willowbrook boys up."

Ms. Ruby went on to explain that the Willowbrook boys were dirt poor, so poor that Clayhatchee's colored residents looked down on them. She said the brothers for some time denied having anything to do with Charles Jr.'s killing, but they never uttered Red's name. Although they were poor and inconsequential, the accused went into court with advantages—the victim was Black, the judge and jury white. The Willowbrook brothers weren't concerned about a conviction until they were convicted.

Ms. Ruby said she will always wonder why those boys decided not to give up Red. As far as she was concerned, no one ever answered for her son's death.

"Katherine, we can't meet like this again," Charles Jr. said, nervously scanning the surroundings.

Charles loved Katherine, but couldn't help but wonder how he had become such a damn fool? He knew being seen with a white girl meant destruction. And yet he couldn't stop feeling for Katherine, the daughter of Red Mansfield, the devil himself. Nonetheless, Charles was determined to end the affair... but she looked so sad, so beautiful.

"I love you Charles, and I can't help that I love you," Katherine said wistfully. The two had been meeting secretly for seven months at old man Withers's abandoned farm. Although it sat on one of Mansfield's properties, the farm was six miles out from downtown, providing them discretion.

"Charles, we could run away."

"Where would we go?"

"Anywhere. Anywhere you wanted to go. I don't care."

"You're talking foolishness, Katherine. You still have a year left of high school. I'm leaving for college."

"I could go with you to Washington. I could finish school there."

"How would we live? What would we do?"

"Charles, I could find work. Doing anything. I don't know. Cooking, cleaning."

"Red Mansfield's daughter working as a domestic. That's something I would have to see."

"All you have to do is take me with you, Charles. And I'll show you. Don't you love me?"

"I love you... too much."

"I love you, Charles. Can't you see this is the only way."

Maybe, it could work Charles thought. They would still have to lay low for now. Although Washington *sat in the shadow of the South, it had to be more accepting than Clayhatchee. They could make a life for themselves. They were both smart, both industrious. And they loved each other.*

"Okay, we'll do it. We can do it."

"Oh, it's going to be so wonderful, Charles. You just wait and see."

The two souls embraced, holding each other tightly. They had hope, and it warmed them. They had a future, and they were blissful. They had a plan, and they felt secure. Wrapped up in their happiness, they missed the lightning and thunder.

"Git your gat damn nigger hands off my daughter," yelled Red, holding Charles by the neck. "I'm gonna keel you, boy."

"Whatever happened to Katherine, Ms. Ruby?"

"I don't know. The girl just disappeared. It broke her mother's heart, but it broke the devil even more. After his wife died, Red became a hermit. I say that had more to do with Katherine than his wife's death or his son's leaving. He fell off the edge of the earth."

"Ms. Ruby, thanks for all of your help."

"You're quite welcome, young man. You be careful. A lot of these old devils are still around, and quite a few young ones, with pitchforks in hand."

"I'll be mindful of that, Ma'am. Thanks again."

As I left her house, I thought about Charles Jr. and the long list of colored boys who had found themselves swinging from a tree in some southern town.

* * * *

It was time to search for the Willowbrook brothers. Were they still in prison, in Clayhatchee? It would be interesting to see how they felt about Red Mansfield's death. Maybe they could tell me who would have wanted to see the ghost dead. I wouldn't be half surprised if Ms. Ruby hadn't put a cap in his ass herself. She's feisty enough. Stranger things have occurred, and she had a damn good motive. But why would she wait so many years for revenge.

Red Mansfield, who had stopped trusting and feeling safe in the world, probably died at the hands of someone he trusted, someone who he felt safe being alone with.

Who killed that damn ghost?

Chapter 13
Stirring up the Spirits

"James, you got a call here from your boss. I left the message on the Frigidaire."

"Thanks, Auntie."

I knew what the chief wanted. He wanted me to file a story. I'd been working on this for the last couple of weeks and hadn't filed anything. But I hadn't found the Willowbrook brothers yet, and I wanted to talk to them first. My goal was to clear my cousin, the article be damned. But I needed to send Chief something. Let me knock something out before I call him.

Old racial wounds don't heal easily in the little town of Clayhatchee, Alabama. When Red Mansfield, who was found dead three weeks ago in his home, was being applauded as a great financial contributor to the city, many in the "African-American" community chose to remember another side of Mansfield. Yes, he was a businessman, yes, he was a philanthropist, and yes, he was an unabashed racist, who spent most of his adult life as a member of the night riders. It's no more evident of hard lingering racial feelings than with Ruby Jackson, who still contends that Mansfield killed her only son, Charles, thirty-seven years ago. Mansfield was never formally implicated in the death of Charles who was found by his mother, hanged. But Jackson maintains that...

After two hours of pounding out my first piece, I went to see Bunky in jail, and he didn't seem well. The bounce, the spunk, the over-the-top bravado was gone from him. He was beyond ready to be home, and I was his only hope. The district attorney's office and the police weren't in a hurry to look for anyone else, which is probably why they hadn't come looking for me. The political establishment wanted to tie this up quick and avoid any huge outside publicity, especially with next year being an election year and the DA running in the gubernatorial race. Bunky's former attorney, the fool who told him to take a plea, wouldn't have been a match for this DA. If Bunky had admitted to killing old man Mansfield, he would have only received a second-degree murder sentence and forty-five years behind bars. Hell, with good behavior, Bunky could be out after twenty years of growing old, disillusioned, and institutionalized. What a deal. I'm glad we found a new attorney.

****

After fruitless attempts to locate the Willowbrook brothers, they suddenly became easy to find. Aunt Dee told me that Jack died ten years ago from "boozing and regrets." As for Roy, he was a big-time preacher.

"All you had to do was ask," she said. "I don't know why you haven't discovered him on yo own… he's all ova television, radio, and da internet."

Before I could respond, Aunt Dee was giving me another hug.

"Boy, you ain't much of an investigative reporter," she laughed.

Roy Willowbrook had a multiracial congregation, almost split down the middle between Black and white. When I called the reverend, I told him that I was working on a story about race relations in Clayhatchee nearly forty years after the civil rights movement. Roy was eager to speak to the fancy reporter from up North. In fact, he invited me to come to his service on Sunday to get a fuller picture of the racial harmony that his church modeled. Roy also offered to have members speak to me about Clayhatchee's transformation from a bastion of hatred and hangings to tolerance and reconciliation. According to Rev. Roy, his community had become a real Kumbaya place, and he couldn't wait to show me how his church was a symbol of the new Clayhatchee.

I wondered if Rev. Roy would have been as eager to talk to me if I had given him my real motive—the death of Red Mansfield. He probably wouldn't have invited me to his church, and I wouldn't have been upset about that. I hadn't been a regular churchgoer since I left home for college. I just didn't have much time for religion or the hypocrites who filled the pews Sunday mornings and the clubs Saturday nights. But the more I thought about it, being in church wouldn't be such a bad thing for me. I needed some spiritual guidance. Hell, I just needed some guidance. I was hopeful that Rev. Roy would offer more than salvation this Sunday morning.

I couldn't get Aunt Dee to go with me to Rev. Roy's church.

"I can't, James. Roy Willowbrook may have found da Lawd, but I don't trust dat man. All I see is two young hellions, him and his brother, always terrorizing Black folks. I wouldn't go to his church even if I was dead."

The Sermon on the Mount Outreach non-denominational church stood in the middle of Clayhatchee as the magnificent monument that it was. The building was less of a building and more of a sporting arena. Layers upon layers of seating. The church had balcony seating, main level seating, lower-level seating. The congregation enjoyed a band on stage equipped with electric guitars, drums, piano, bongos, and tambourines. Movie-size screens were placed on both sides of the pulpit to enhance the viewing of those in the back. Keeping with its racial harmony theme, none of the traditional white Jesus pictures you saw in white churches and none of the traditional Black Jesus pictures you saw in Black churches were hung or painted in this coliseum. The congregation created quite an impressive picture all on its own—a collage of Black and white folks, sweating, singing, praying, praising, crying, yelling, and worshiping together as one.

And right in the middle of it all was Reverend Roy Willowbrook holding court and promising fire and brimstone to anyone who didn't repent. Rev. Roy looked unlike what I had pictured. Even after talking to him on the phone, I still had in my mind some skinny white punk with acne, attitude, and animus. But the man I saw up there commanding the congregation was not the Roy Willowbrook my Aunt Dee described. This Roy oozed affability—a round affable face to go with his round affable body. Roy Willowbrook wasn't a puny punk at all. He was a gargantuan man, standing about six feet two inches tall and weighing more than three hundred pounds. He appeared to be in his late fifties. And just like many other men his age, his balding process was just about complete. As pleasant as his face unnaturally was, it became recognizably disagreeable when he warned parishioners not to fall into the devil's pit of seeking earthly treasures, earthly satisfaction, and earthly salvation. Rev. Roy's long black robe, accentuated and exaggerated his violent arm movements and his affable body no longer seemed friendly, now appearing as a weapon he could summon at any moment with powerful effect. The reverend slashed his arms, cutting the air as he spoke to an eager, hungry group. He filled the pulpit. The pulpit looked too small for him as he walked back and forth offering admonitions.

"A man chasing fool's gold is just a fool, setting himself up for hell and damnation," Rev. Roy said, to a chorus of "Amen" from the rainbow denomination.

"We need to look to build our treasures in Heaven. You can't take these earthly treasures with you, and Heaven's treasures won't rust," Rev. Roy almost sang to another chorus of agreement. "You can bury them in the ground, but that's where they'll be, in the ground. Don't bury yourself. Stand up for what's eternal, what's beautiful. Can I get y'all to stand up for your salvation, a salvation that's eternal? Stand up and turn away from your life of sin and earthly pursuits. Stand up now!"

And they stood. And they came. Most of them, with tears in their eyes, dutifully went to the front of the church to touch Rev. Roy and receive the promise of salvation. White, Black, young, old, about twelve in all, heeded the reverend's warning and were saved as the choir sang "Amazing Grace."

At the end of the service, I asked a young Black usher, appearing to be in his early twenties, sporting two hoop earrings and cornrows and the typical white gloves and black suit, to lead me to Rev. Roy's office. We walked down a long-narrowed hallway passing three other offices.

"Pardon me, Rev. Roy. I have that reporter from New York. Are you ready to see him?"

"Oh, yes. We can't keep our northern friend waiting. C'mon in," Rev. Roy said, pumping my hand and slapping me on the back as I entered his princely office. "How are you doing, Mr. Kingsman? What can I do for you? What do you want to know about the new South? Do you want to know how there's been a spirit of reconciliation and forgiveness and redemption not only in Clayhatchee, but throughout the entire South? I'm sure we could give you Yankees a tip or two about race relations, Black and white living in harmony."

He continued to pump my arm and smile at me the entire time. This guy was going to be a tough interview.

"I'm sure you can," I said, "but that's not exactly what I want to talk to you about. I want to talk about Red Mansfield. What can you tell me about him, and who do you think wanted to kill him?"

Rev. Roy stopped smiling, shifting his large body uneasily in his desk chair, engulfed by a majestic mahogany desk. A desk that appeared to be suited more for a CEO of a Fortune 500 company than a reverend of a southern church.

"Mr. Kingsman have you fibbed to me? I thought you were a newsman. You're not FBI or some other law official?"

"No, I am who I say I am. I'm a reporter from New York who wants information about Red Mansfield. What can you tell me about the man and his enemies?"

"I haven't talked to Red Mansfield in years. Unfortunately, he wasn't a regular here at The Sermon on the Mount. It's also unfortunate that the old man could not die peacefully, strung up like some old farm animal."

"From what I understand, Red wasn't a peaceful man," I said. "You live by the sword and you die by the sword. Isn't that in the good book?"

"Turning the other cheek is also in the Bible, Mr. Kingsman. There's no doubt that Red was a hell-raiser in his younger days from the stories I've heard growing up, but Red hadn't raised hell in years. He was what you call a recluse. He didn't bother anyone, and no one bothered him, until recently. I'm not sure what I can tell you about this man that you haven't heard from other people."

"Well, can you answer this? Why did you and your brother take the rap for killing that Jackson boy?"

Rev. Roy's eyes bugged out a bit as if this were the first time he had ever heard his name associated with the death of Charles Jackson Jr. With a meaty hand adorned by rings, the reverend wiped dirt and sweat from his pudgy face. When he was done with his self-cleaning, Rev. Roy leaned forward to make his point clear.

"My brother and I paid our debt for poor Charlie. God rest his soul."

"That may be the case, but some people around here believe that the only reason you and your brother went to trial was to conceal Red Mansfield's involvement in poor Charlie's death. How did Red Mansfield get you involved?"

Rev. Roy pushed his office chair away from his desk and stood up. While he was leaning over his desk, he began to point toward me. The affable preacher of reconciliation façade evaporated, and I came face-to-face with my first redneck since coming to the South.

"Listen, here, Yankee, you're barking up the wrong tree. I'm not sure what you're after, but you're not going to get it from me. So, you can get the hell out of my office," he said, raising his voice.

"Rev. Roy, I'm sorry for any inconvenience. I'll be on my way. Here's my card if you want to talk later. I am still interested in talking about racial harmony and forgiveness with you," I said, dropping my card on his desk and turning to walk out of the door.

What a fruitful meeting. I now knew Rev. Roy had something to hide. A man who acts that defensively always has something to conceal. What did Mama always say about throwing a rock at a pack of dogs? Oh, yeah, "A hit dog will holler." Rev. Roy was hollering for sure.

Even so, Bunky was still suffering because of my inability to get any closer to the truth.

Chapter 14
Meeting M

Two days passed, and I was still thinking about my meeting with Rev. Roy. Why had he become hostile? What nerve had I struck? I knew he had more information, and I needed it now. Bunky's preliminary hearing was a day after tomorrow. As a reporter, I attended many of these hearings, more formality than anything. The prosecution presented enough of its case to have the trial occur, while the defense sat mute, except to ask for all the charges to be dropped for one reason or another. Every prelim I witnessed went to trial. I didn't picture it going any differently.

As the hearing approached, Aunt Dee became Ms. Busybody—sewing, cooking, gardening, and thinking. She also asked me a lot of questions, including why there even needed to be a preliminary hearing.

"It's to see if the prosecution has enough evidence to have the case heard before a jury of his peers," I said.

"Well, first of all, it's not gonna be no jury of his peers. A Black man in Clayhatchee has neva gone befo no jury of his peers. The only decision dat judge is gonna make is to have my boy face a trial."

To that, I didn't reply. She was right. I had viewed the system in action—brothers being led into the system, brothers in the system, or brothers returning institutionalized from the system. Often, they faced a white courtroom, with a white judge, a white jury, and white attorneys. Many times, the defendant, the victim, and both families were Black.

"Aunt Dee, we don't know. Maybe, Bunky's attorney has found some type of loophole."

"My boy don't need no loophole. He needs justice. He's innocent. He told me he didn't kill dat man and dat's good enough fo me. Oh Lawd, I just wants da truth to come out. Bunky is a lotta things, but we knows he ain't no killa. My boy is no killa."

As predicted, Bunky's preliminary hearing came, and his case was held for trial, without much of a fight from Geckman, who undoubtedly was holding back his best stuff for the trial. With Red Mansfield's prominence, an election around the corner, and the racial ramifications, Bunky's case was fast-tracked. His trial was set for two months from now.

It was dark when I finally got back to Aunt Dee's house. No doubt she was exhausted and had gone to bed. As I made my way up the steps, I decided to redouble my efforts to find the ghost slayer. I would make another trip to the good Rev. Roy. I would scour through court documents to see what was still out there. I would talk to the police about the crime site, which would not be easy. An arrest had been made, and as far as the police were concerned, they had their man, case closed. Police, in general, were tight-lipped, suspicious people by nature. They would be even more suspicious of an outsider, who just happens to be a reporter, who just happens to be from the North. Nonetheless, I was planning to hit Clayhatchee's finest tomorrow, trying to throw around as much weight as my press badge could muster.

As I was plotting my strategy, Aunt Dee informed me that a letter had come with my name on it. The handwriting was neat—like a woman's scrawl—with no return address. The letter read:

Dear Mr. Kingsman,
You don't know me, but I believe that I can be of some help to you. If you like, we can meet at the Crestwood Estate Bed & Breakfast on Bush Run Road. I have reserved the drawing room. Let's plan to meet tomorrow at noon.
M

M? The same M who paid for the funeral.

"You sure da letta said Crestwood Estate?" Aunt Dee quizzed. "Dat place was sold and torn down years ago. Let me look at dat note."

I handed it to Aunt Dee. She grunted and handed the note back to me.

"It says Crestwood Estate all right. Take Buford Road until it intersects wit General Lee Avenue. Den take Birmingham Street til you run into da old Patton stow. Make a left on to Bush Run. You should run right into da Crestwood Estate. At least dat's where it was. Good luck."

Aunt Dee directions were perfect. She was right about everything except the part about Crestwood Estate. Yes, indeed, the Crestwood Estate still existed, and it was grand, antebellum-like. It didn't take much to picture balls, great balls, grand balls, debutante balls in this structure. The building stood erect, a pillar of fine southern society. I grew apprehensive as I went to ring the doorbell. I hesitated a bit, wanting to flee but not knowing why. I rang the bell.

The door opened and it was my M, the white woman I had seen at Mama's funeral. She was prettier than I remembered from that day. In fact, she was outright gorgeous. She didn't wear a hat, allowing me to notice her hair. She had a curly wild mane. Dark huge curly locks that fell easily on her shoulders. Seriously, her curls seemed to prance on her shoulders, framing her face perfectly. Her white skin had an olive tone to it, accentuated with light freckles. Her eyes were bright green, and her nose was pointy but flared out at the nostrils. She had thin lips yet with a fullness about them. She was exotic looking. I had placed her in her fifties when I first saw her, but now face-to-face, I couldn't tell her age. Nothing gave it away—not her hair, her shapely curves, her eyes, her mouth, her voice.

"Mr. Kingsman, please come in," said the grinning white woman, who seemed to lean in to give me a kiss or a hug, but thought better of it. Instead, M shot out her hand for a firm shake on her part.

As wonderful as the mansion appeared on the outside, it was magnificent inside. It had marble floors, white marble pillars. It had a long winding rail that went up three flights of stairs. A water fountain sat in the middle of the floor, next to a Zeus statue.

"Mr. Kingsman, may I interest you in something to drink?"
"No thanks, and you may call me James. What may I call you?"
"Let's just wait on that for a minute."
"Okay, but can you at least tell me why I'm here?"

"I'm sorry that's going to have to wait as well, honey. However, I have some questions and issues that need to be cleared up by you first. Did our cousin Bunky kill Red Mansfield?"

"No!" *Did she say...*

"Did you kill Mansfield?"

"No," I blurted. "Damn, nothing like being direct."

"Sorry for my bluntness," she said, "but I needed to know before we moved on. You confirmed what I had already believed to be true."

"Did you say Bunky was *our* cousin?"

She smiled, looking directly into my eyes.

"My name is Mildred Mansfield Freeman. I used to go by Katherine Mansfield. I knew your mother well."

Katherine Mansfield? The ghost's daughter?

"How and why would you know anything about my mother?"

"Because she was my mother. She was our mother."

Chapter 15
Killing Daddy

"James, I've known of you for years. I've watched you grow, and I've listened and read about your accomplishments. You've grown into an impressive young man. Mama was proud of you. I'm proud of you."

Was this white woman crazy?

I just stared, and the more intently I looked at her, the more her features gave way to Mama's.

"Red Mansfield was my father," Mildred blurted out. "He raped our mother, and I was conceived."

What? My brain suddenly stopped working. I needed to sit. Was I already sitting? The room spun and colors flashed, and her words pounded my skull.

"After Mama had me, she gave me up for adoption," she continued, although I was still lost at *raped our mother*. "Mama thought she was giving me away to some well-to-do Black family. Mama's midwife lied to her and, instead of placing me with a Black family, sold me to a white family, to Red's family. The midwife thought she could fetch a good price for me from some barren white woman because I appeared white. She was right."

"This is a lot to process," I said. "How do I know what you're saying is true. Is there a birth certificate?"

"James," she said, "a midwife, no hospital, and a quick adoption would not produce any true record. I do have a birth certificate, and it names Red and Victoria Mansfield as my parents."

"And that would say Katherine?" I responded, with a strange trace of rudeness. "But that's no longer your name?"

"Call me, Mildred. And it's complicated, James."

"Make it simple for me, Mildred."

"Okay, James."

Mildred told me she was Victoria Mansfield's "miracle" child. In 1947, Victoria had suffered some complications during the birth of Robert E., both almost dying. The doctor said she wouldn't be able to have any more children. It was devastating to Victoria Mansfield, who had always pictured a home filled with many children, especially a little girl she could love and train in southern lady ways. Seeing her depression, Miss Victoria's maid, Bunche, suggested her mistress go to Bottom Hill and talk to Ora Lee DeVough, a mystical Creole woman in her sixties from Louisiana. Some Black folks thought old Ora Lee could heal anyone of anything.

"She healed Victoria with a baby girl—me—in need of a family."

Mildred placed her hand on mine.

"I was an adult when I met Mama. I was nearly grown when I found out my mother was not my birth mama and my father was… I understand your shock. Think of my reaction when I found out I wasn't who I thought I was… that I was conceived through violence. As difficult as this is for you to process, well, you understand."

"When exactly did you find this out and how? When did you meet Mama?"

Mildred had a cigarette in one hand and a drink in another as she moved around the room with a purposeful aimlessness. She offered me a drink, but I quickly declined (Why? I don't know. I needed a drink). She sat down, looked at me, and began her story.

"I found Mama in 1973, and we've met often and secretly over the years. I made the trip to Pittsburgh. Your father wasn't about to let her go back to Clayhatchee by herself, and she never planned to set foot back here as long as your father was alive. Through the years I came to know you, Frances, Mark, and Cecilia through Mama."

"Again, when and how did you find out all of this?"

"Well, James…"

Mildred started from the beginning, telling me she spent her childhood worshiping and trying to please her father. To the despair of her mother, Victoria Mansfield, she could be just like Red, even more spiteful. But Red's animosity was deep; she realized hers was surface. Everything changed for Mildred when she fell in love with Charles—up became down, down became up, black became white, white became black and Mildred became undone.

Charles was the most beautiful boy she had ever seen. His eyes touched her first, those deep piercing brown eyes. He had been working around the family mansion for about a month when Mildred finally looked into his eyes—the first time she had really examined a colored person's face. His doe eyes caught her, and his tan skin emerged magnificently. She saw beauty and intelligence and poise and confidence and kindness and goodness. And she knew Charles had to be avoided, so when they did speak, she made certain the social constructs were in place—she was Miss Katherine, and he was Charlie. She was his employer, and he was her servant. She was white and he was not. And with gusto, she went out of her way to let him know his place, but more so to remind herself. Katherine was abrupt, curt, condescending. And then she tripped.

While walking home, Katherine stepped into a ditch, severely spraining her ankle. Hearing her scream, Charles rushed to her, and without thinking, gingerly picked her up, wrapping her in his arms, pulling her close to him, and carrying her home while comforting her the entire time. That's when order changed for Katherine Mildred Mansfield. Her vision became clear. She finally *saw* Charles.

At first, that *seeing* allowed Mildred to engage in polite small talk, which evolved into longer and deeper talks. She saw his character, his intellect, his being, and she saw his heart. And she did the unthinkable, she loved him. And through Charles, something amazing happened— she saw others.

Mildred and Charles guarded their secret, making plans on how they could escape Clayhatchee. They would go up North and marry; people were a little more liberal about those things, so she had been told. They had it all figured out. She would work while Charles finished his medical degree at Howard. Once he was finished, she would go to college. They would both work until she had children. They thought the plan was sound and felt a confidence in their furtiveness. And then everything changed.

Deciding one evening to take the long way home to assess the value of the abandoned Withers's farm, Red happened upon Charles and his daughter. Sensing something off, Red fought himself and stayed put and listened. And in his stillness, he raged inside as confessions were uttered. The moment Charles embraced Mildred, Red pounced. Mildred said that Red would have killed Charles if it hadn't been for all of her crying. She begged her daddy to spare Charles and promised never to see him again. Mildred saved Charles, she thought.

> *My daughter, acting like common white trash. I can barely look at her. I'll send her away to school, and then I'll deal with Charles Jackson. How dare that nigger touch my daughter, touch a Mansfield. That little nigger needs a lesson. The Willowbrook boys will help. It would be better to keep some distance.*

Mildred was inconsolable. She was disillusioned. Although Red was never charged and was steadfast in his denials, Mildred knew what her father had done. After Charles's death, Red was dead to Mildred. She told her mother she was leaving Clayhatchee and would not return until Red was in the ground.

Mildred never wanted to leave her mother. Victoria explained to Mildred that the love she felt for Charles was not wrong or unnatural. It was then Victoria confessed that she was not Mildred's biological mother; that her mother had been a colored woman and her father a white man. Mildred had more inquiries than Victoria could keep up with. But Victoria could not give Mildred the name of her biological mother. Nor, could she tell Mildred that Red was her father and that she was conceived and raised by a rapist. Victoria had always had an uncanny feeling that Red and his daughter had a bond that was more than incidental, and learned the truth from the midwife, Ora Lee.

Mildred, on her last stop out of Clayhatchee forever, made the same truth-seeking visit to Ora Lee.

> *"Now, child, what do you need from Miss Ora Lee?"*
> *"Who's my mother and father?"*
> *"Miss Victoria and Mr. Red."*

CARLISLE

"No. Who are my real parents? I was told my mama's colored and my daddy is a white man."

"You sho you want to dig up those old ghosts, mistress?"

"Are you sure you don't want to go to jail?" Katherine shot back. "I wonder what the statute of limitations is on selling babies?"

Ora Lee squared her body to look Katherine in the eyes. "You as mean as your father, Red."

"Red is not my father."

"But he is, child. Red be your daddy and Pudding Williamson your mama. Your cracker pappy raped her," said Ora Lee, now stirring a wooden spoon in a huge clay-like bowl.

Katherine tried to find somewhere to sit. Why did HE have to be her real father? She had not only lived with and loved this man, but she also had worshiped him... this rapist.

At that moment, Katherine stopped being white. She forever disavowed Red's white blood running in her veins. She would live as a Black woman.

"Did my mother know?" Katherine asked, barely loud enough to be heard.

Ora Lee put down the bowl. "She didn't know for years that Red was your father. But she found out..."

"How do I find Pudding Williamson?"

"I'm a poor old midwife."

"Would $350 help?"

"I can't help you find a Pudding Williamson, but I think I can help you locate Mrs. Elaine Kingsman."

After Mildred left Clayhatchee, she began shedding her old self on her way to discovering her new self. She found out her biological mother had started a new life for herself in Pittsburgh. Elaine and John Kingsman had raised four children. She had settled in as a housewife and her husband a laborer in the steel mill. They had migrated into a community filled with Black expatriates of the South, trying to make a living for themselves free from the outright, unforgiving racism and discrimination. Their children were attending integrated public schools.

"When I was a student at Howard, I contacted Mama for the first time," Mildred said. "I wrote her a letter."

"You went to Howard?"

"It's where Charles wanted to go. I went for Charles and in doing so, I found myself."

"What did you find exactly?"

"I found I was a Black woman, what it meant to be a Black woman. I found pride in having a Black mother, having a Black existence. I tried to cut myself off from my past. I started going by my middle name Mildred, my grandmother's name. Katherine was part of my past now. Howard allowed me to discover myself and in doing so, gave me the impetus to find Mama. I found her address and wrote her a letter."

"What did Mama do after receiving your letter?"

"She wrote me back, the first of many letters. I loved getting letters from her. I loved her handwriting—so precise, so pretty, so loving."

James noticed, for the first time, Mildred was crying softly. The more he stared at Mildred, the more she looked like their mama. She even cried like Mama, fidgeting with her fingers, sighing loudly between soft hums. Yes, this woman was his sister.

"Mama asked me to forgive her. But, forgive her for what? I told Mama she didn't do anything wrong, and I told Mama I loved her. Mama was easy to love. Mama said she never stopped loving me. I was fortunate to have a special relationship with her for thirty-one years."

"Why didn't Mama bring you to the family?"

"What do you think your father would have done?"

"Because of Red?"

"James, I didn't give a damn about Red, and Mama didn't either. But she did care about John Kingsman. She didn't want your father to suffer through any more indignities."

"My daddy would have been able to distinguish between you and your father. Mama should have had more faith in him."

"She did. I asked her not to say anything. I didn't think it was right to disrupt your family and bring the baggage of Red Mansfield along."

"So, to that regard, Mildred, you had a motive to kill Red?"

"Yes, I did. And every day he was alive, I killed him. When I left his house, I killed him. When I cut myself out of his life, I killed him. When Victoria told Red I was partly colored, I killed him. I killed him when I married my wonderful Black dark-skinned husband, Herbert Leon Freeman, God rest his soul. I killed Red. I have spent most of my life killing Red Mansfield."

Sister Mildred had made the case of who killed the ghost more complicated, but I needed to focus. I needed answers.

"I'm back to square one, trying to figure out who killed Red. From what I can surmise, many people would have been happy to bury a steak knife into his back. Yet still, I have no more leads and this case appears to have gone cold for me."

"Not quite. Have you met Sterling Clemons?"

"No. Why? Who is he?"

"Go see him. He is my father's longtime lawyer and is handling the estate. There is a lot of money tied up in all of this."

"Do you think someone killed your father over money?"

"I don't know, but an ace reporter such as yourself should be able to find something out."

"Why didn't you ever come by after my father died?"

"We were moving toward that when Mama died."

Mildred started crying again, and I instinctively went to her and placed my arm around her. She was, after all, my big sister.

"Thank you for fulfilling Mama's wish," she said, "and bringing her back home. Mama said she could always count on you."

"It's time for you to meet the rest of the family, Sis."

> "You drove my baby girl away. Just like you drove Robert away. I don't know if my sweet boy is dead or alive or if I'll ever see him again. I'll never forgive you for taking my children away from me," Victoria screamed at Red. "Your children didn't fit your image of yourself. Well, Red, as sissified as Robert is, he is more man than you'll ever be.

"And you want to know something else, Red? Your baby girl, the one you adored, and drove away, she did nothing wrong in the sight of God's laws or man's. As God is my witness, she is as Black as that boy Charles Johnson Jr. Katherine is Pudding Williamson's child. Pudding gave up her baby all those years ago to my midwife, Ora Lee, after being raped by a white man; after being raped by you."

CARLISLE

Chapter 16
Been Dead

I met with attorney Sterling Clemons. At first, it seemed like a waste of a meeting. All he would divulge was public information. I did learn some things. Although Red lived like a pauper in his later years, he was still an extremely wealthy man, worth millions. I guess Mildred would inherit his money. Mildred's brother, who had taught English at a small liberal arts school in the New England area, was rumored to have died in a car accident about ten years ago.

As I was wondering why Mildred sent me to the lawyer, he told me about a will. Red had requested that I be present during Friday's reading of the will. This was all very strange.

Leaving one attorney's office, frustrated yet intrigued, I received a call from Bunky's lawyer. Paul Geckman said charges were being dropped and Bunky was being let out of jail. Forensic evidence determined Mansfield had been killed two days before Bunky entered the home. At the time, Bunky was spending the night in the county jail for unpaid parking tickets, of all things. This is the one time his dereliction kept him out of trouble. Fortunately, Bunky hadn't told anyone, including his lawyer that I had been in Mansfield's home. The autopsy officially determined Red died of asphyxiation by way of hanging. The ropes had been pulled so tight they had cut an inch into Red's old pale skin. The approximate time and day of Red's death are what got Bunky's butt off the hook. He had a solid alibi. If Bunky's public defender had done a little work, my cousin would not have sat in jail as long as he did. Thank goodness for Geckman.

Geckman said other items, which he was not privileged to divulge, indicated Bunky could not have been the killer. Bunky had concocted some half-baked story for why his prints were found in Red's home and the trespassing charges were dropped. Since nothing had been stolen, the police had no way of proving the cash wasn't Bunky's. Geckman said Bunky needed a ride home, and I was more than happy to oblige.

This story was growing more interesting by the moment. Mansfield was lynched in the same distasteful manner suffered by scores of Black men through the ages. I needed to send Cuddy an updated story about the case. Should I tell him anything about Mildred? Probably not. Should I tell him about the reading of the will? No. I'll keep those items to myself for now. I'll give Cuddy the police report story.

"Glad your cousin is free. So, when will I have your next story?"

"Chief, you might pretend a little harder that you're concerned about my cousin."

"Look, James, my job is to run a newspaper. Your job is to provide stories for my newspaper, so when am I going to get this next story?"

"I'll have it to you tonight."

"Now that's the ace reporter I know and love. Have you heard anything else?

"What do you mean?"

"What do you mean what do I mean?"

"Nothing."

"Nothing. As in you have nothing else to say or that you haven't heard anything else?"

"I have nothing else to give you now, but I'll keep you posted."

"You do that, James."

"Always a joy, Chief."

I needed to call Aunt Dee to tell her I was bringing Bunky home. She would be ecstatic her baby was coming home, and he hadn't done anything wrong, so to speak. Yes, good news. My mind was racing. I needed to call Jackie. But first Aunt Dee. Her phone message picked up, and Aunt Dee's voice blessed me as a caller, and I heard the gospel sounds of the Soul Stirrers in the background. Leave a message. I didn't. I'd make my way to the county jail, a quick thirty-mile jaunt, and have Bunky home in ninety minutes. Geckman had most likely taken care of processing the paperwork. I was merely a ride. Television and print reporters would probably be there, and I was sure Geckman planned to hold court.

I liked Geckman, and I was grateful for his efforts to free my cousin, but I knew his type, had seen it often when I covered the courthouse beat. He was flash-and-bulb, never missing an opportunity to stand in front of a camera. Maybe, I should have left a message telling Aunt Dee that Bunky was coming home today. She might see the news before I get him home. I wondered why Bunky wanted me to come get him from jail rather than his mother or one of his women. Maybe, he just needed to talk to me alone. What I learned about my cousin in this brief time was he always had a reason for doing something. He didn't move unless there was an angle. I would find out soon enough. No need to worry. Instead, as I drove, I decided to call Jackie. She would calm me, give me her insights. Good, she was home.

"Hey, baby."

"What's wrong, James?"

"Wrong? Nothing is wrong."

"I hear it?"

"Hear what?"

"I hear something deep in the back of your throat."

"What, you have a stethoscope?"

"Stop playing with me, James. Tell me what's on your mind."

"I have good news. Bunky is being released. I'm on my way now to get him."

"That's great news. Did they find out who killed the old man?"

"Not yet, but the district attorney had no case because Bunky had been sitting in the county jail for unpaid parking tickets at the time of Mansfield's death."

"Why was Bunky in the man's home at all?"

"No longer an issue."

"Is there something wrong?"

"I have an older sister."

"Yes, James, you do. Her name is Frances. Nice lady. She gives you hell."

"No, this sister is older than Frances; she came before Frances, and she's white, sort of."

"What?"

I told Jackie the entire story, not stopping until the reading of will on Friday and Red Mansfield had wanted me to be present.

"You do plan to be there?"

"I don't think there is anything that could keep me from the reading."

"Do you trust this Mildred character? Have you checked her out?"

"She's my sister."

"How do you know?"

"I just know."

"When do you think you'll be back?"

"Soon, but..."

"But what?"

"Jackie, don't you have some vacation time?"

"I might."

"You've never been down South? It's beautiful down here."

"That's what I hear."

"I'm feeling lost and confused."

"What is it, James?"

"It's you, me, the will, my mom, this place, everything."

"Let me make some moves here, make some arrangements. I'll be there."

"I love you, Jackie."

"I know you do. See you in a day or two."

With that, she hung up her phone. She still wasn't giving me an inch, but Jackie was coming to Clayhatchee.

Chapter 17
Bunky's Revelation

Surprisingly, when I arrived at the jail there was no Geckman and no media. He must have made some other arrangements with the press. No way he was going to miss a moment to shine. Nonetheless, it was just Bunky looking on nonchalantly as if he were waiting for a bus to arrive and not as a man who just beat a murder rap. Bunky held the drawstrings of a clear plastic bag filled with clothes dangling over his right shoulder. He smoked a Newport while leaning on a wall, looking at nothing in particular. He barely shifted his body as I pulled up to the curb. Casually flicking his cigarette butt (who cares about a littering fine when you just beat a murder rap), Bunky strolled toward the car, opened the front door and tossed his bag in the back. His big smile revealed the gold tooth in the corner of his mouth.

"I have some news for you, but let's get out of here," Bunky said, as he searched for some dirty South hip hop on the radio.

Without a word, Bunky played with the dials on the car radio. We listened to Outkast's "Player's Ball" for a few seconds then he switched to Ludacris' "Stand Up" for another thirty seconds before settling on Juvenile's "Back That Azz Up."

"I heard in the joint that the white cracker was worth millions," Bunky said, eyes still focused on the radio.

"Is that your big news? I already found that out."

"That's not it."

"What else?"

"I was approached by these two white boys in the joint. They asked me how much I got for offing Mansfield."

"What did you say? Please tell me you said nothing? You think it was a setup?"

"Cuz, I've been around long enough to know when to keep my mouth closed. I just listened to them. They wanted to talk. Ski-Ball said he and his brother Low-Low, those white boys ain't never been bright, were approached about offing Mansfield. Low-Low said they had been offered $25,000 each."

"Are you saying those white boys killed Mansfield?"

"They say they didn't. They said they weren't trying to do that type of time, no matter how much money was being offered."

"Who made the offer to them?"

"They wouldn't give any names. They did say she was some old rich white broad."

"Do you believe this Ski-Ball and Low-Low? And why would they give you that much info about themselves?"

"They gave up info because they were fishing for some. Plus, those mutha fuckers just ain't that smart. Dumb white boys. They don't make crackers down here like they used to. Whatever information they told me, they probably already provided to the DA. Both of them are in the joint for long drug convictions. They are trying to get their out-of-jail pass."

"So, the police are looking for this white woman now?"

"They should be, but these aren't the brightest law enforcement officers in the country either."

"Did Ski-Ball and Low-Low give you any other details about the white woman?"

"Nothing except she was fine."

"Fine is relative when you're in jail."

"Ain't that the truth?"

My mind was racing again. An older, fine white woman? My new sister fit the description. No, it wasn't her. No…

* * * *

We went straight to Aunt Dee's house, but she still wasn't home. Where could she be? Did she know Bunky was out of jail. There had to be something on the news. Geckman, I'm sure had his news conference by now.

We drove to Bunky's main home. His wife and children were crying, while they kissed and hugged him. For all the coolness he displayed earlier, it was gone for Bunky as soon as he entered the door. He immediately started crying when he saw his family, and then he laughed, and he couldn't stop laughing. He seemed at peace. Bunky and Gloria invited me to stay for dinner, but I declined. I started to ask if she had heard from Aunt Dee but decided to just go home. Maybe Aunt Dee would be in her chair when I walked in the door. I had more thinking to do.

Why would these white boys provide that much information to Bunky? Was it true? If so, who was this white woman and why would she want Mansfield dead? Again, could it be Mildred? Granted I didn't know my sister very well, but she didn't appear the type to make hit offers, but what did I know.

Three more days until the reading of Red's last will and testament. Maybe it would provide some answers to this puzzle. Lord knows I hoped so.

As I approached Aunt Dee's house, I noticed the lights were on. Good, she was home. When I walked in, Aunt Dee was drinking lemonade with Mildred, my sister. They sat in a familiar way, and they both looked up and smiled.

"Hello, James," Mildred said, as she put her drink on the coaster and squared her body to view me directly.

Before I could respond, Aunt Dee rushed to me with arms open.

"Bunky is outta jail. Thank you, James. Thank you so much, chile. I knew my baby was innocent. I prayed to da Lawd dat my baby would be set free. Praise da Lawd! I thank da Lawd fo you, James."

"Ah, Aunt Dee, " I gasped from inside the hug. "No, the good Lord deserves all the credit."

"The good Lawd does, but he used you as his instrument. You always believed dat yo cousin was innocent. You helped find him a good lawya. I thanks da Lawd, but I thanks you too, nephew."

"You did a great job, James. You did right," Mildred said, still smiling.

Aunt Dee finally let me go and sheepishly smiled at Mildred. Before I could step back, Aunt Dee grabbed my arm, pinching it slightly, while smiling all along.

"I see you have finally met your sista, Milly. Isn't she lovely, James? Dis just warms my heart. I wish your mama was here. Her dream was always to unite Milly wit da rest of da family. James, it's up to you. Dat's what yo mama wanted. Dat's why you're here."

I looked at my aunt and then at Mildred and they both seemed to be in sinful delight of knowing a secret.

"How long have you known, Auntie?"

"About your sista?"

"Yes, my sister, Mildred, Milly, M, Katherine," I said, half-jokingly. "Any other aliases?"

"I've known fo years. I've known as long as yo mama has known. When she found out bout Milly, I was da only person she could tell. She wanted me to look out for Milly anytime she came home to Alabama."

"Why did the two of you act like complete strangers at Mama's viewing? And, Aunt Dee, you feigned ignorance about the flowers sent by M? Did everybody know this secret but me."

"Yo mama thought it best," said Aunt Dee.

"I know, for Daddy's sake. Mildred told me."

And then it was quiet, the three of us seemingly stuck inside an uncomfortable silence.

"Aunt Dee," I finally blurted. "Did Mildred tell you that, at first, I suspected she might be Red's killer."

"Lawd, James, she's your sista!"

"But I'd only known her a couple of minutes. Now I trust her. But if I was a police detective, I might wonder if she killed him or had him killed for the inheritance."

"Stop it, James."

"It's okay," Mildred said, as she stretched out her arm to pat Aunt Dee's hand. "James knows I didn't place a hit on my daddy. Regardless of how insufferable he was, I still loved the bastard. Excuse me, Aunt Dee."

"You forgiven, child."

120

CARLISLE

Truth according to Mildred was that Red doted on his little girl and she basked in his attention. He became her protector, her guardian. And she loved her daddy. Softened him up a bit, as much as anyone could. Still, both were cut from the same cloth. Then, she viewed Blacks through the same lens as Red. To hear her tell it, she embraced her South and its traditions—segregation, discrimination, and racism. She had little empathy for the Black folks in her Clayhatchee community. And while she garnered her daddy's affection, she drove Victoria crazy. She was Red Mansfield's child, through and through. Her brother, not so much.

Robert E. Mansfield had his mother's sensitivity and sense of fairness. Robert E. developed a more open and radical idea of Black Americans. As a young boy, he befriended many of the Blacks in town. Robert understood the color line, but still retained those friendships through high school, much to the outrage of his father. Immediately after high school, Robert E. left Clayhatchee for a northern college to get as far away from Red as he could.

"Robert E. was a sweet boy," Aunt Dee seemed to say to no one in particular, and without concern for interrupting Mildred.

"As far as the money," Mildred continued, "I don't know what's going to happen at the reading of the will or if I'm even included in his will. We were estranged for the most part. Besides, I've been pretty well to do for years. I'm very comfortable. I don't need or want Red's money. Never did."

"I believe you," I said, although the back of my mind still had some questions.

"You better believe yo sista," Aunt Dee commanded.

With that, Mildred finished her lemonade, stood up from the chair, and gave Aunt Dee a long embrace. Mildred looked like my mother hugging her big sister. Uncanny.

"I love you, Aunt Dee," said Mildred. "It's always wonderful seeing you."

"I love you too, chile. You make sure you see me fo you leave Alabama, Milly."

"I will," she said, turning to wink at me. "James, I'll see you Friday."

I nodded and gave her a hug. Life had become so confusing.

Chapter 18
They Here

I was running. I was running through high grass and weeds. I heard dogs barking. I heard voices. Men. Men speaking loudly. The louder the voices became, the more frantically I swiped, thrashed at the tall weeds. The louder the voices became, the faster I ran. I violently swung my arms from side to side, brushing away the high grass, becoming more furious with every new sound. I reached a clearing. I could see beyond my arms. I was coming upon a body of water, a river. I saw Jackie on the other side. "Hurry," she cried as the voices behind me grew louder. I heard heavy feet and quick hooves trampling the ground. The voices had become clearer, more audible. "Get him," came a scream from a blare of haunting white mass. "Get his nigger ass!" And I heard Jackie. "Trust me. Come in the water. It will be okay, James. Come in the water, James. It will be okay, James. Come…"

"Jackie?"

"Come on, James. I'm here, baby."

"Jackie?"

"Wake up, baby. It's me. I'm here."

"Is it really you, Jackie?"

"It's me, and I'm at the airport."

* * * *

I jumped out of bed, still not sure if I was awake. Jackie was here. She'd help me make sense out of all of this mayhem.

As I was rushing out of the house, Aunt Dee told me that Frances, Mark, and Celia were flying in this evening for the reading of the will on Friday. How did they even know about it? Aunt Dee said all three of them had been contacted and told they needed to be here. Knowing them, they probably believed they were in for some money, a lot of money, or none of them would have had the gumption to make arrangements and fly themselves to Clayhatchee. I know my family. I thought it curious that all the Kingsman children had to be here for the reading of Mansfield's will, a man none of us knew, a man Mama loathed, and a man Daddy would have killed if he weren't already dead. Normally, I would have been pissed that they were coming, since they couldn't make it to Mama's second funeral.

Strangely enough, I was comforted by the thought that my family was going to be here; even if Frances was bossy, Mark an intellectual snob, and Celia just plain silly for her age. With Mama gone, we were really all we had, well, including Mildred. Did they know about Mildred? No, they couldn't know. I wondered what they would think of our new big sister. I still wasn't sure what I thought, but something inside kept me from discounting her. She loved our mama. Those feelings were real. Yes, it was going to be interesting to see how the northern clan was going to welcome Mildred. Frances might crack, finding out she's no longer the oldest. I wondered what Jackie would think of Mildred? Jackie had an uncanny knack for sizing people up quickly and correctly.

I was feeling something that I hadn't for a while, happy—good about family, good about Jackie, who looked stunning as ever.

Jackie had already retrieved her two bags. As she searched for me, she didn't notice I was nearly in front of her. I didn't mind. It gave me a chance to take her all in; she was like sunshine after a hard rain. She filled up any room with her presence. She always got me going. Her dark skin seemed to always have a luster to it. Jackie was regal in appearance, speech, and action. She was an African queen. My African queen. She kept her hair short, Toni Braxton like. Her jewelry clang harmoniously; large silver bracelets on both wrists, a silver necklace around her neck, and a silver ring on her finger. She liked the way silver clashed against her Black skin. So did I. Magnificent.

"Ma'am, do you need help with those bags?"

"Well, I was waiting for my strong handsome friend to give me a hand. Have you seen him?"

"Yes, I saw him leaving."

"Well, I guess you will do."

And with that, she flung her body on me with so much force, she almost knocked me over. She wrapped her arms around my neck and soulfully kissed me. The kiss felt life-sustaining. I needed more of her, more of her lips, her breath... her life. I needed her to breathe her life into my body. I needed her. I needed her to be my family. I was ready.

"You missed me."

"You don't know how much. I'm glad you're here, girl."

"I am too."

We spent the drive from the airport catching up. I had only been gone for a month, but it had seemed like an eternity. And from what I could tell Jackie, felt the same way. She missed me. But was she ready to forgive me? I hadn't realized how lonely I had become until I made this trip down South. I didn't want to be lonely. I didn't want to be by myself. I needed Jackie and, strangely, I needed my family.

"Is Mildred beautiful?" Jackie asked.

"Yes, she reminds me of my mother when she was young."

"Does she act like your mother?"

"No. In a strange way, she seems more like Daddy. She has a toughness about her. But even with Mildred's hardness, she's charming and sweet. She's also polished and an intellectual."

"When will I get to meet this new sister of yours? She seems fascinating."

"I was hoping you would say that. I can't wait."

Chapter 19
The Family Gathering

Aunt Dee was preparing for a feast, combining an out-of-jail party for Bunky and a family reunion celebration for her northern kinfolk. The house smelled of southern deliciousness—cornbread, black-eyed peas, fried chicken, okra, sweet potatoes, and greens. Aunt Dee was wearing her apron and doing her thing. As captain of her kitchen, she was providing direction and encouragement to her daughters (Sherry and Alice), Bunky's baby mama (Lori), and his wife (Gloria). The space was at capacity. As soon as Jackie and I walked in the door, Aunt Dee stopped what she was doing, and without missing a beat, she seemed to skip to us until she was in reach to give Jackie a long motherly embrace, even though the two had never met.

"Why have you not married dis fine Christian woman?" Aunt Dee kidded.

It was amazing how easily Jackie clicked with Aunt Dee. Mama too had immediately fallen in love with Jackie. Those two had become fast friends. Mama was a bit perturbed with me for letting Jackie slip away. "Don't give up hope," Mama had said to me. "Jackie is just what this family needs."

After some brief introductions, we went into the living room.

"Red Mansfield wants da entire family at da readin' of his will," Aunt Dee said. "I hope dere's a bomb-sniffin' dog. Dat dead old Red might try to take us all out."

Aunt Dee was laughing and jiggling, finding herself amusing. Far-fetched, but not really. I couldn't fathom why Red Mansfield wanted my family at his will reading. None of us knew him. What could he possibly be leaving us? In fact, all he had ever done had been to take from my family—

stripping Mama of her innocence, keeping my parents from their home, taking our sister from us. Did he want more from us?

"I guess the mystery will be revealed tomorrow," I said, looking at my aunt. "And then it's back home for us."

"Home? You already home, James. Have you thought bout makin' dis place yo home? It would be nice to have at least one of Puddin's children in Clayhatchee."

"What do you think, Jackie? Should I make Clayhatchee home?"

"Home is where the heart is. Where does your heart reside?"

"I don't know."

"You don't know?"

"I don't know."

With that, Jackie turned her gaze to Aunt Dee. She was done with our conversation.

"Aunt Dee, could you show me where my room is for the night? I'd like to unpack my things and freshen up a bit before the entire family arrives."

"Of course, dear. Where are my mannas? Yes, honey let me show you to yo room. You be real comfortable. I put you in da room with da ceilin' fan. Right dis way. James, get Jackie's bags."

"Don't worry about it, James. I can get my own bags," Jackie said as she followed Aunt Dee.

"No woman will be carryin' bags around in my house," Aunt Dee said, looking at me. "James, bring Jackie's bags up."

I watched as they ascended the steps. I hadn't been around Jackie but a hot minute, and I had already seemed to have pissed her off. How do I do these things? And what does she mean home is where the heart is? My heart is with her, but home is a different matter. I had always said I was leaving Pittsburgh the first chance I got, and I did. I never truly had a kinship with the city. It was too small, too homogeneous, and still too racist. Even now, the neighborhoods still resembled early 20th century communities steeped in enclaves of nationalities—the Italians owned the South Side, the Irish and Polish had the North Side, the Jews ran the East End, and the Black folks had the Hill and every other depressed neighborhood. No, beyond the sports teams, there was little attachment to Pittsburgh. It never had my heart.

New York was sexy, but she could be too big, too complicated, and at times, too much for me to truly call home. I did have an affinity for New York, but it was more about work than the city itself.

Clayhatchee? Home? No, I couldn't see it.

"Jackie's settled in," Aunt Dee said. "She's takin' a shower."

"Thanks, Auntie. Thanks for taking care of her."

"You welcome, James, but my guess is Jackie would like you takin' care of her mo den me."

"I want to, it's just..."

"It's just 'nothing', James. Dat's a fine woman. When you find a fine woman, you promise to take care of her, and you spend da rest of yo life livin' up to dat promise. Life can be difficult, but a good woman can ease yo path. And dat woman is a good woman. You hear?"

Aunt Dee was right. My lifelong fear of commitment was the block that I stumbled over with Jackie. I was trying to get back up, even more so since coming to Clayhatchee. Somewhere between burying my mama and this murder drama, my fear of commitment had been overtaken by my fear of being alone, growing old by myself. I didn't want to die like old man Red, alone and mostly forgotten. I didn't want his fate. I knew now more than I had ever known that I wanted Jackie to be in my life forever. I wanted Jackie to be my wife. I needed her to be my wife. Before we leave Clayhatchee, I would tell her I was ready to take the next step and beg her to take me back. Would she be ready to forgive and trust me? She just had to.

Family was still arriving in droves. Children and grandchildren, nieces and nephews, cousins and more cousins filled Aunt Dee's house and the house came alive. Aunt Dee didn't go for all of that rap music nonsense, as she called it, but she allowed Bunky to indulge since it was his get-out-of-jail party. He blasted Master P's "Make 'Em Say Ugh" throughout the house. I met Cousin Lester, Cousin J.P., Cousin Lucy, and her three children (LaShan, Laqueda, and LaRon). I met Cousin Fred and Cousin June Bug, Cousin Boo Bear, Cousin Honey, Cousin Luke, and all of his children from Mattie. It was a madhouse. The music rapidly looped from rap to old funk and gospel. Children were dancing and playing and running around. Grown folks had plates and liquor... talked loudly, laughed, and had fun. And Bunky, as always, was holding court.

"I kid you not. This fat old white security guard, he had to be in his late sixties, asked me if I could provide him the hookup."

"Get da hell outta here. I don't believe dat," said Cary Johnson, one of Bunky's homeboys.

"No, real talk, man. He said he was trying to supplement his income and needed my help. I asked why he come to me? He said some of the other inmates had been talking about me and told him I had the bomb shit. You know I got a rep. You know I'm legendary around these parts."

"What you do, jigger man?" asked Leroy Benson.

"What you think I did, Leroy? I put him on the payroll."

"Are you outta yo damn mind?" Cary interjected.

"Hey, no cussing over dere," Aunt Dee yelled as she stopped her conversation to correct a group of grown men.

"Sorry, Aunt Dee," Cary said before going back to Bunky and asking in a lowered voice, "Are you out *of* your damn mind?"

"No. I needed to make my stay work for me, and I saw this fat white security guard as my hook up. You know if it's not going to help me, I'm not going to do it."

"But how do you trust security?" Cary asked.

"I don't trust. But I've dealt with folks like this guard. The trick is, find out what a person desires, what he wants."

"So how does that work out for you?" I asked, finally getting up the nerve to chime in this conversation.

"Fabulously. The guard is one of my best business associates."

"How you know he's ain't gonna roll on you?" Cary asked again.

"Cary, you're not letting up. He's not going to roll because he wants that pension. He's been at that job for twenty-two years. He's trying to reach thirty years and retire. He's not gonna lose all the time and money put into his career to dime me out. I have him."

"Sounds like you have each other," I said.

"Well, my business is a tangled web."

"You need to be careful not to get caught in the net," I said. "I'll be out of here later tomorrow."

CARLISLE

"I know, Cuz. Let's talk later."

I nodded my head and turned. My baby was walking down the steps. She was joining the party. Damn, Jackie looked good. Damn, she made a brother proud. As she sauntered down the stairs, she seemed to have the room. Center stage had left Bunky. My chocolate honey was working it. As she reached the bottom of the steps, I grabbed her by the hand. And as soon as she hit the bottom step, Bunky was the first one greeting her.

"So, this is your city girl, Cuz? You got a good eye. I'm cousin Bunky. What's your name, sweetie?"

"Jackie, and it's nice to meet you, Bunky," she said extending a hand out to Bunky, who ignored it.

"Naw, girl. We hug and kiss around here," Bunky said as he pulled Jackie into him, a little too close for my comfort, but it was Bunky.

Jackie looked surprised.

Cousin Willie also wanted a hug.

"Hey dere," Willie said to Jackie.

Bunky pulled Jackie away.

"Leave this pretty woman alone," he said to Willie, laughing.

"Whad?"

"Don't sass your uncle," Bunky interrupted before Willie could say another word. "I don't care if you are two years older than me."

Willie shyly smiled at Jackie and headed to the kitchen.

"That was Willie, my nephew," I heard Bunky whisper to Jackie. "Gal, let me in introduce you to the family."

I let them go and watched as he moved from person to person with my girl. Jackie now looked amused. Later, she was outright laughing as I could see Bunky's mouth moving rapidly. Jackie was good. I was good. Bunky was a good dude. I liked him. I liked him a lot. He just had to get out of those streets. His luck wasn't going to last forever. Bunky finally brought my girl back to me. They both seem to be in good cheer.

"Here she is, Cuz. I think I introduced her to everyone. Y'all enjoy yourself. You have a fine woman. You got a good one."

"Thank you, Cousin Bunky," Jackie said, leaning and kissing him on the cheek.

"Fine woman. Mighty fine woman," Bunky said as he went back to holding court with his boys.

"Looked like you enjoyed yourself with Cousin Bunky."

"He's hilarious and a sweetie."

"He's a good dude. He has a lot more depth to him than he shows."

"I can believe that," Jackie said, grabbing my hand.

"He needs to get out of his lifestyle before it catches up to him. You know, like a lot of brothers, caught in a system without many options and locked away when they make the wrong choice."

"I know," she said. Of course, we all knew.

"He wants to talk later," I said, "so I might try to talk some sense into him. I'm not sure it's going to help."

"It can't hurt."

"How about with you?"

"What about with me?"

"Talking."

"I like to talk."

"I know that well. But do you like to listen?"

"Depends on what's being said and by whom. A woman is particular."

"It's me doing the talking. I have something to say."

"Say it, James."

"Marry me."

"What?"

"I said, marry me."

"And why would I do that?"

"Because you love me. Because, at one time, you wanted to marry me."

"I'm dealing with that problem."

"It's not a problem."

"It's been a problem for me. What else do you have?"

"I love you."

"You loved me before. But neither your love nor my love was good enough. You chose you, your career, your skank, and your fear of commitment."

Oh, yeah, those things. I grabbed her other hand.

"Jackie, nothing matters without you. The time here has allowed me to get my priorities straight to see what really is important. Family is important. You are important. Spending the rest of my life with you would make my life important. It would give me meaning. I love you. I'm ready."

"Are you really ready, James?"

"I've never been more ready."

"I see. But I'm not ready."

She made her statement without blinking an eye. In fact, she looked me straight in the eyes, not intimidated by hurting my feelings. I was sunk. All I could do was muster a feeble question.

"When will you be ready?"

"When I'm ready."

"That's not giving me much."

"I know."

"I'll wait."

"We'll see."

Just then, Aunt Dee marched over. Her timing was reminiscent of my mother. Aunt Dee walked like my mother, or maybe my mother walked like Aunt Dee. I wasn't sure. I hadn't noticed that they were similar not just in walk, but in appearance as well. Aunt Dee's flamboyancy tempered with her gruffness must have kept me from seeing the resemblance—the walnut-shaped eyes, the narrow thin nose, and the long curly hair. Although Aunt Dee had outweighed my mother by nearly a hundred pounds, that notwithstanding, they really looked alike and, by extension, my sister Mildred looked like both of them.

"Where yo brotha and sistas?" Aunt Dee quizzed. "Dey should be here by now. I don't like to worry."

"Aunt Dee, I'm sure the plane was late or something. They'll be here."

"Well, how you two doin'?" Aunt Dee asked. "Jackie, you need anything, baby?"

"She won't marry me," I interrupted, "but other than that, we're fine."

Jackie blushed a bit. I'm a jerk sometimes, I know.

"We're fine, Aunt Dee. Thank you."

THE SOULS OF CLAYHATCHEE

"Maybe she won't marry you cause you keep answerin' fo her," Aunt Dee instructed. "It probably wouldn't hurt if you'd use some of dat Kingsman charm. She's a keeper."

"I'm trying."

"Try harder."

"I will."

"Jackie, James is a fool; just like Bunky, just like Bunky's father, just like men in general. But he's yo fool, and he'll be yo loyal fool fo life. We need mo smart women in dis family."

"Well, thank you, Aunt Dee," Jackie said, laughing.

"Aunt Dee, is Mildred coming?" I said, trying to change the subject.

"No. Milly called and said she wouldn't be able to make it."

"That's unfortunate. I wanted Jackie to meet her."

"I'll get to meet her tomorrow."

"It won't be the same. You won't have much time to talk to her. Plus, when the hearing is over, we're gone."

"Well, she felt bad bout missin' family."

"Family?" I blurted.

"James, you don't give yo sista nuff credit," Aunt Dee scolded.

"I just call it as I see it. I don't think she knows anything about our family."

"She put you through college."

"What?"

"It's true, James. When yo father was laid off from da mill, money was tight, so much so dat da savings put away for yo college had to be used so da family could make it until yo daddy's pension and social security kicked in for y'all. Dere was no money for you, and Milly offered to pay yo way. Yo mama didn't even have to ask her. In fact, she tried to decline da money, but yo sista would not take no for an answer, and she went and paid all four years of yo tuition. Milly was so proud when you graduated."

"I thought I received a minority scholarship. Was my guidance counselor in on this as well?"

"Probably."

"What a wonderful gift," Jackie said, finally able to cut in.

"Why would she do that? She didn't know me, nor did she know anyone beyond you and Mama."

"Because you are family," Aunt Dee said. "She loved yo mama and she loves her family. She knew yo potential, how well you did in high school, and all those activities. She was happy to help you reach yo goals."

"Did Daddy know?"

"You know yo prideful daddy didn't know. That's why yo mama made it look like a scholarship."

"I'm going to pay her back every cent."

I wasn't sure why, but I was offended. All along I thought I had earned a scholarship and made it through college on my own merit. Now I find out that my rich white sister paid for my education.

"I'm paying her back."

"James, I don't think she wants or needs yo money, but you do what you feel you have to do. I was just tryin' to show you dat Milly knows da meanin' of family."

With that, Aunt Dee moved over to where Bunky was still jabbering to his boys. Not missing a beat, Bunky put his arm around his mama and continued to tell dirty jokes, and I'm sure I saw Aunt Dee laughing. Jackie moved closer to me, putting her fingers on the back of my neck as if she was preparing to kiss me.

"Why the attitude, James?"

"I don't know. It just seems Mildred was meddling in my life and I didn't even know she existed."

"She did a good thing for you," Jackie whispered in my ear while still rubbing my neck. "You know, James, if Mildred hadn't paid your college tuition, we wouldn't have met. For that alone, she's high in my book."

"Maybe, you're right."

"Mama's always right."

"I need you tonight, Mama. Since you won't marry me, you think we can have some good old-fashioned out-of-wedlock sex?"

"I think that's called fornication and no, absolutely not in Aunt Dee's house. Go to bed, James. You need your rest for tomorrow. I need my rest as well. I'll see you in the morning."

The party wasn't quite over, but people were beginning to leave. My

brother and sisters had still not arrived... and now I was a bit worried.
"I love you," I said as Jackie climbed the stairs.
"I love you too, Mr. Kingsman," Jackie said, without looking back.
Later, I made it to my bedroom. It was dark.

"I'm begging you. Please don't kill me."
The white man cried out as he kneeled in front of the six-foot black giant. His fire-red hair seemed to be in stark contrast to his white skin that had gone pale. The man's voice cracked as he wept. John Kingsman had the shiny silver knife at the white man's neck with one hand and a fistful of his hair in the other hand. He had beaten Red Mansfield almost beyond recognition and was about to end his life.

John had always hated this cracker, the punk who thought Blacks should all kowtow to him. Not John. Never. He didn't know how to kowtow to white people, the yessum and no ma'am. Mansfield knew that about John and jumped at any chance to taunt him. Both knew one day they would have a reckoning.

"You ain't shit," Kingsman said.

"I swear to you J.R., I never touched your woman. I knew she was your girl. I'm a married man."

"Petey Smalls and Bakerfield Smith sang a different tune," John said as he sliced the knife down from Red's right ear to the corner of his mouth, blood flowing from the gaping cut. Mansfield yelled out in pain.

"You're one dead motherfucker," John grumbled as he lifted the knife.

"Stop, J.R., leave him be," Dee yelled. "White folks are looking for you. We need to get you outta here."

"If I ever see you again," John threatened, pushing Red as Dee pulled him away. As the two turned north running full speed, Red rolled on the ground, trying to stop the blood with his hands.

Dee promised John that she would get her sister

CARLISLE

to join him when he was settled in a safe place. John vowed to never return. He didn't know that his future bride was with child. That she was having Red's baby.

Chapter 20
No Po Po

I woke up ready for this day to start and end. How strange a dead cracker summoned my entire family to be at the reading of *his* will.

Although I was glad Bunky and I weren't in jail, I still had a gnawing need to know who killed the bastard. If we could discover the woman who tried to get the two white boys to off Mansfield, Bunky and I could go to the police with the information. Maybe the DA would strike a deal with Low-Low and Ski-Ball, or whatever they called themselves. We might finally find out who was behind Mansfield's death. I'm sure Mildred wanted to know who killed her father. Maybe I could get Mildred to go to the police. They would take her seriously. Bunky needed to tell Mildred what he told me.

"Are you crazy?" Bunky asked, looking at me incredulously.

"No. I'm not crazy. Don't you want to clear your good name and see that the real killer is found?"

"First of all, I don't have a good name. Second, I have an alibi and I'm out of jail. And third, I don't give a damn about dead ass old Mansfield."

"You don't care about finding the truth?"

"Let it go, James."

That was the first time he called me by my first name since I arrived in Clayhatchee.

"Why should I, Bunky?"

"Cuz, what good is going to come out of it? I've already sat in jail over this bullshit. Do you want to go to jail?"

"How is that going to happen? I didn't touch that man."

"I didn't touch him either, but I was in jail waiting to go on trial for his murder. Lucky for me I have an airtight alibi. How about you, stranger? Do you have an alibi, Mr. Big City Man?"

"I didn't kill that man."

"Look, James, you and I know you didn't kill that man, but a jury full of crackers don't know that. In fact, I'm surprised no one has come to haul your Black ass off to jail already. You come to town and the man is found dead. If I were you, I be heading back to New Yoke as fast as I could. Hell, I don't even know if I would stay for the will. Well, maybe, if I thought there was some money coming my way."

"Okay, Bunky, I hear you. But would you care if someone else went to the police about those white boys?"

"James, I'm telling you not to go there."

"I'm not. I was thinking about having Mildred Freeman go."

"Who is Mildred Freeman?"

"Mildred Mansfield Freeman is Red's daughter," James said.

"I didn't know he had a daughter. Why would his daughter speak for us, James?" Bunky asked.

"Because in addition to being Red's daughter, she's my sister and your first cousin. She's the result of the rape."

"Hell naw, what? Are you for real?"

"Yes, I'm for real. It's true. She's my sister, your cousin. Aunt Dee has known this for years."

"I wish I had known. I would have hit her up for money years ago. Let's go see my rich cousin."

Bunky didn't seem to be approaching this in the manner I had hoped he would.

I hadn't seen or talked to Mildred since the revelations. I was disappointed she hadn't made it to Aunt Dee's. I wanted Jackie's opinion about Mildred, but more than that, I wanted Mildred's approval of Jackie. I'm not sure why. Crazy. When we pulled up to Mildred's home, I could see her through the window, dressed in a robe. Bunky noticed as well.

"You sho she's kin?"

"Your first cousin, Bunk. Chill."

"Damn, that's too bad. She's fine."

Mildred swung open the door with a grace worthy of a ballerina.

She appeared genuinely happy to see me. And I felt a warmth toward her. I stopped being mad that she paid for my college education, and I began to feel grateful and silly for my initial reaction. I noticed, yet again, how her features blended with Mama's. This woman was indeed my sister. If I had doubts before, I didn't now.

"Hello, James. I didn't think I would see you until the reading. Come on in."

"Hi, Mildred. This is Bunky."

"I know, Aunt Dee's son and my cousin. Welcome to my home, Bunky. I'm glad you're out of jail. I never thought you killed my daddy," she said, in a matter of fact sort of way.

"Mildred Mansfield. It would have been good to know you were my cousin when they carried me off to jail. I could have used your juice."

"What won't change," I interrupted, "is that your daddy's killer or killers are still out there."

"Red Mansfield was dead a long time before he was killed. You couldn't call what he was doing living," Mildred said, looking away in thought.

"Nonetheless, he was breathing," I countered. "We have some information that could help solve your father's murder."

"Take it to the police, James."

"Because he was your father, we thought that you might be interested in any additional information. You do want your father's murder solved, don't you?"

"What do you have, James?"

"I don't have anything, but Bunky does. Tell her, Bunky."

"While I was in the joint, two white guys I've known for years told me they had been approached by a white lady to kill your daddy. They asked me if I had been approached by the same lady."

"Were you?"

"I can tell you without a doubt that I was not approached by a white woman, at least not to kill Mansfield."

"Did they give you any more information about this white woman?" Mildred asked.

That seemed funny coming from Mildred's mouth. Although I accepted that she was my mother's daughter, I still hadn't thought of her as a Black woman. However, for the first time, she came off like a Black woman, questioning Bunky about that "white woman." Surreal. Most definitely surreal.

"They didn't have a name, or they weren't giving me a name," said Bunky. "I think they just wanted to see what I knew. I'm not even sure if they were telling the truth. Dem niggas like to lie."

"We were thinking about having you go to the police with this information," I said interrupting.

"Go to the police with what?"

"We have two white guys who said they were approached by a white woman to kill your father. Isn't that enough?" I asked.

"You have nothing, James."

"You don't think that the police would want to question these guys?"

"No. If these men had something for real, they would have had their own lawyers talking to the police trying to make a deal or something. I would stay clear of the police and this trouble."

There she goes again, looking white but sounding more and more like a Black woman.

"That's what I told him," Bunky jumped in, nodding his head affirmatively. "Maybe New Yoke will listen now."

"You two are probably right," I said.

"I know," Mildred said.

"Why do you think your daddy wanted my entire family at the reading of his will?"

"That's as much of a mystery as his death. I guess we'll find out later today. Honestly, I don't know."

"One more question, and we will be on our way. Why did you pay for my college?"

"Because you needed money to go to school, you're my brother, and Mama desperately wanted to see you become a college graduate. She wanted that more than anything. I was in a position to help, so I helped, and I'm proud of my investment."

"Thank you. I'll pay back every cent."

"You're welcome, but you don't have to pay me back. It was a gift."

"It was too generous of a gift. I'll pay you back."

"No need. The gift wasn't just for you. It was for Mama as well."

* * * *

As we left, I couldn't help but wonder why Mildred didn't seem more concerned about finding her father's killer. And how did she reconcile who her father was, who her mother was, who she thought her mother was, and who she thought she was? How did she acknowledge that she was a product of a violent rape and her daddy the rapist? How could she be so nonchalant about his death? Mildred was unlike anyone I had ever met, but there was a familiarity. I did like her. And I was going to pay her back regardless of what she said. It might have been a gift to Mama, but I was the one who directly benefited.

"Are you going to go to the police?" Bunky asked.

"No. If Mildred isn't concerned about finding the killer, why should I care? We're good. I can live with that."

"Now, you're talking like you have some damn sense, Cuz."

"Even so, didn't you think it was strange Mildred's lack of concern about her father's death? She seemed to have a coldness about it. I don't understand."

"Maybe, it's not for you to understand, Cuz. I'm sure she's been trying for years to sort out her feelings for her father. I'm sure part of her doesn't give a damn that Red is dead. She's probably ready to move on."

"I guess. After the reading of the will, we all can move on."

"Right again, cousin."

When I walked into the house, Jackie and Aunt Dee were sharing coffee and laughing. What a nice picture. I hadn't been noticed, which gave me a chance to just watch. They looked like two girls sharing a secret as they both alternated crouching in to hear the other better. They both were dressed for the big event. Aunt Dee appeared as if she were stepping out to go to church. Jackie, however, was dressed for a meeting, business as usual.

Aunt Dee place her hand on top of Jackie's hand. And I saw a tear roll down Jackie's face. Why was she crying? Should I ease back out or interrupt this intimacy? Before I could decide, Jackie spoke.

"It's not polite to spy on people," she said, wiping her eyes.

"I wasn't spying."

CARLISLE

"Boy, how long have you been there spying on us?" Aunt Dee asked.

"I wasn't spying. What's wrong?"

"Nothing is wrong. We were having a wonderful conversation."

"So, why the tears, babe? Are you okay?"

"Aunt Dee was showing me pictures of your mother. I was just thinking about how good your mother was, and I got emotional. Nothing is wrong."

"James, you're not much of a spy," Aunt Dee said, chuckling.

"I wasn't spying."

"Where have you been anyway? You need to get ready," Jackie said.

"I was with Bunky, and we went to see Mildred."

"You saw, Milly? And you took Bunky? You know she's never met him before," Aunt Dee said with a bit of exasperation.

"I know. I thought that was a bit strange since you've known Milly for years."

"Why did you and Bunky go over to Milly's?" my aunt now asked firmly.

"We had some information that we wanted to share with Mildred, but she wasn't interested."

"What was the info?" Jackie chimed in.

"Bunky said two white boys came to him while he was in jail and said that they had been approached by a white woman to kill Red."

"Did he give you the names of the white boys? Did he know the white woman's name?" Jackie quizzed, sounding a lot like Mildred.

"He had nicknames for the white guys, but he didn't know who the white woman was."

"What good do you think that little bitty information would be to Milly?" Aunt Dee asked.

"I thought she might be able to go to the police with it," I said.

"Go to the police with what, James?" Aunt Dee blurted.

"I'm not sure. Mildred has pull. It was her father who was murdered. The killer is still out there."

"James, what we have is divine retribution," Aunt Dee said. "Red had it coming."

"James, I think Mildred had the right idea," Jackie added. "No need to borrow trouble. Let's just go to the reading of the will and get home."

THE SOULS OF CLAYHATCHEE

The last time Red Mansfield stared at death John Kingsman was standing over him with a switchblade. If it hadn't been for that Dee, he would have been a goner. But now, Red was certain he would die.

But hadn't he changed his ways? He hadn't messed with a colored in years. Didn't he allow the maid to stay on years after her usefulness? Didn't he give the reverend money to help with his multicultural church? Hadn't he made amends to Elaine?

Sweet Elaine. He had wanted to make things right with her, with everyone he had hurt. A lifetime of regrets raced through Red's mind as the chair beneath him was kicked away.

Chapter 21
The Big Payback

At the county courthouse, Judge Wilford Simmons was scheduled to conduct the proceedings. Now in his seventies, Judge Simmons, had been on the bench since 1955, witnessing the transformation of the South—and America—through his steely stare and devotion to law. He was a rare bird; a man who was loved, hated, feared, and respected. He took a no-nonsense approach to law and did not suffer fools or unprepared lawyers in his courtroom. Even in his advanced age, the six-foot-five judge was an imposing figure.

I had spoken with my sisters and brother on the courthouse steps. Their plane was delayed and didn't arrive until late last night. Not only did they miss the party, but to the protestation of Aunt Dee, stayed at the Clayhatchee Days Inn. Frances, Mark, and Celia appeared rested and eager. They were in the dark as to the drama that had unfolded, but their faces revealed hopeful anticipation. Maybe they did some research on Mansfield and figured their big payday had finally arrived. To my great surprise, I was overjoyed they were here. I did love them, no matter how much they got on my nerves.

In addition to my family, a thin white woman, full of edges and angles, sat stoned face. With one hand on the top of a black leather briefcase, the woman stared straight ahead, not speaking or keeping anyone's glance. She had the look of a person who didn't want to be bothered, all business. I wondered if she represented the estate.

Just before noon, Mildred ambled into the room, looking stately. She was dressed in a pinstriped blue jacket with a matching skirt. Frances, Mark, and Celia perked up and looked at Mildred as she made her way to the front of the courtroom. The one thing I finally did was tell my siblings about our oldest sister, and although they had not met her, there was a sense of knowing amongst them when Mildred walked into the courtroom. Mildred bent down and kissed Aunt Dee before exchanging pleasantries with Jackie. Bunky was not in attendance, having proclaimed he was not walking into another courtroom if he didn't have to "no matter how much cheddar was at stake."

Mildred excused herself and made her way to our sisters and brother, giving each of them a hug.

"I am delighted to finally meet you," she said. "Mama told me so much about you and your families. I'm hopeful that we will get the chance to know each other better."

They all sat silent, none of them sure with what to say. But then, former big sister spoke.

"We sure will get that chance. Oh, my lord, she looks just like Mama. Please, sit. Mildred. Sit right here with us," Frances said.

Watching the family reunion, I didn't notice the older white gentleman who trailed Mildred. The man looked tentative as he made his way to the front.

"Alfred, come here. Here's a seat for you," Mildred said, signaling her attorney to the table in the front of the courtroom that sat across from the stone-faced woman.

The courtroom door swung open one more time and to my surprise, Ms. Ruby slowly walked in with the help of a cane and a young Black man. As soon as the clock struck noon, Judge Simmons walked in, we stood up, were told to be seated, and the proceedings started.

"We are here to read the official last will and testament of Robert John Lee Mansfield. I assume all the interested parties are present along with legal representation."

"Your honor, I'm Alfred Studenbaker, and I am representing the estate, Mildred Mansfield Freeman, and I would be willing to represent the Kingsman family, if there's no objection," said the little attorney, who was now standing.

None of us objected. I don't believe any of us had even considered seeking legal counsel for this hearing. We just assumed that it would be routine, but then again, nothing had been routine since I arrived.

Even before Studenbaker sat down, the hard-looking woman full of angles stood up. Ann Stealthman said she was an attorney and her client had an urgent interest in the reading of the will. Ms. Stealthman did not reveal her client but sat down as quickly as she had stood and, again, looked straight ahead—cold, unemotional, calculating. The young Black man, next to Ms. Ruby, stood up and introduced himself as Harold Ford, legal counsel to the local chapter of the NAACP.

"Let's begin," said Judge Simmons, looking down at the document. "Dated February 1, 2001, Robert John Lee Mansfield, being of sound mind and body, has bequeathed sixty percent of his estate and holdings to his only known living heir--formerly Katherine Mansfield now known as Mildred Freeman. In the event that his only son, Robert E. Mansfield, is alive, he and Katherine will split the sixty percent in half."

The judge paused for a moment, then continued.

"The deceased has included a note," he said. "To Katherine, my beloved daughter, I know you will do more good with this money than I ever could. You've been blessed with the traits of the mother who birthed you and the mother who nurtured you. I am sorry for my many failures."

I looked over at Mildred, who seemed to be crying. Frances handed her a handkerchief and patted her on the knee. Frances then put her arm around Mildred and Mildred did something I did not expect. She placed her head on Frances' breast. I watched my sisters who had just met, appearing as if they had shared a lifetime together.

"To the family of Charles Jackson Jr., I bequeath your family thirty percent of my estate. I know money will never bring back Charles Jr., but I hope it can help heal the wounds left from the past. I take full ownership for the killing of Charles and Ruby Jackson's son. I will go to my grave with that regret. I am not asking for your forgiveness because I do not deserve it. But I do want to tell you how sorry I am."

Mildred let out a large gasp as if she had been struck in the gut. She seemed to fold over continuously, becoming smaller with each fold, and then she started sobbing louder and uncontrollably. Ms. Ruby started crying and praying at the same time. She tried to stand up, raising her arms with her palms facing up as she looked past the ceiling toward the sky.

"Thank you, Jesus. I finally know the truth about my boy. I must forgive you Red because God has forgiven me. Maybe he will have mercy on your soul, Red Mansfield," Ms. Ruby said still staring at the sky beyond the ceiling, completely oblivious to the judge, furiously banging his gavel.

"Counsel, please get your clients under control," Judge Simmons said.

"Sorry, your honor," young Ford said, putting an arm around Ms. Ruby and gently guiding her back to her seat.

"If there are any more outbursts, I will stop this proceeding. Do you understand?" Judge Simmons asked, scanning his courtroom. Counsel for all parties nodded their heads in collective agreement.

It appeared to be my family's turn. We were finally going to find out why the ghost had summoned us. I was almost certain that old Red had not left the remaining ten percent of his estate to the Kingsman family. After all, John Kingsman did try to kill him. I wouldn't argue that he didn't owe my mother, but I didn't have him paying up. No, he called my family here for one last indignity. I couldn't be as forgiving as Ms. Ruby. My hope was Red was being stabbed with a pitchfork. There was nothing he could have written, said, or done to change my mind on that.

"To the family of Elaine Kingsman, our families are linked through my daughter Katherine, Mrs. Mildred Freeman. She was conceived through my horrible sin. I will never be able to justify my actions. The only comfort I can take is Katherine's birth, and for that, I will always be grateful to Elaine Kingsman. I know none of this will undo what I've done and how I lived. I will have to answer to my maker for Charles, for Elaine, and for many, many others, but I lived in a different time, in a different South. Perhaps if I had been born forty or fifty years later, I would have been a better man. Being of sound mind and body, I do bequeath to the descendants of Elaine and James Kingsman my home, all the contents within, and the remaining ten percent of my estate. Please accept my gift, please accept my apology, and please, above all, accept my daughter as kin."

Mark was shaking, Celia was praising Jesus, Frances was chuckling, and I was mumbling (softly to myself). I was dumbfounded, not by the money, but by Red's Coming to Jesus moment. Hearing by his own admission that he respected my mother was not only confusing but also galling.

Almost immediately, the sounds of my family members gave way to the voice of attorney Stealthman, who was now speaking for her mystery client.

"Your honor, if I understand correctly, there have been no provisions made for my client, the Rev. Roy Willowbrook. My client, who had a relationship with Mr. Mansfield for years, had been promised along with his now-deceased brother monetary compensation at the time of Mr. Mansfield's death. I have documentation."

A chorus of objections reverberated throughout the courtroom.

"All counsel please approach the bench," Judge Simmons said, somewhat annoyed again.

The judge nearly snatched the document out of Stealthman's hand. Judge Simmons read the piece of paper to himself, he handed it to the other two attorneys to read and had them return to their respective tables.

Judge Simmons read the document aloud.

"Being of sound mind and body, I, Robert John Lee Mansfield, bequeath all of my earthly belongings to Roy Willowbrook on this day June 16, 2004. Signed by Robert John Lee Mansfield and witnessed by attorney Ann Stealthman." Judge Simmons placed the document down and stared at Rev. Roy's attorney.

"My question, Ms. Stealthman, is why are you now just submitting this document to the court? What was your reason for holding on to it?"

Attorneys Ford and Studenbaker couldn't get to their feet quickly enough. Surprisingly, the older Studenbaker, maybe because of more practice, was swifter than Ford, and he was objecting and requesting that the new claim be dismissed because of the lateness of the document to the proceeding.

"Wait. I want to hear from Ms. Stealthman," Judge Simmons said.

Stealthman, as stone-faced as she was when she entered the courtroom, seemed unfazed by Judge Simmons' slight admonition and clear annoyance. In fact, the attorney acted a bit annoyed by the judge.

"Your honor, I just assumed this would be the will that you would be reading from since it had been submitted prior to this hearing. You should have already had a copy. As you can see, this document is the rightful will. It has been signed, witnessed, and notarized. I'm not sure what type of fraud is being perpetrated on this court, but my document is the true will of the deceased."

"I again request that this court dismisses the Rev. Roy's claim," Studenbaker demanded. "The documents were not entered in time, nor properly. There is no time to even examine if the document is legitimate. It all appears fishy to me, your honor."

This time it was Stealthman angrily objecting, jumping to her feet while pushing the chair back with her thighs.

"I am deeply offended, your honor, by the implications being raised by counsel. This document is indeed legitimate, and my client has the rightful and only claim. I request that the court consider this will, verify its veracity before making a final decision."

"I will review both documents and make a decision in three days," Judge Simmons growled. "This court is dismissed."

With that, Judge Simmons banged his gavel, stood up, and disappeared into his chambers, leaving us all baffled by the turn of events.

Jackie and I walked over to my siblings, sharing expressions of surprise and shock.

"Alfred, what do you know about this Ann Stealthman?" Mildred asked.

"Not much, but I'll see what I can find," Studenbaker said.

"We're not getting any money?" my brother asked.

"Not today, it appears," I said.

As I grabbed for Jackie, who reached for me, Stealthman walked past us and out of the courtroom without a word. I felt the reporter in me resurface, and he had many questions: Who was Ann Stealthman? How did Reverend Roy weasel his way into Mansfield's entire fortune? And why did the reverend neglect to let me know of his arrangement when we spoke? Oh yeah, I forgot, he barely knew Red Mansfield

CARLISLE

when I went to talk to him a few weeks ago. Should I go back to the good reverend? When was this going to end? I kept thinking about what Bunky had said about those white dudes being approached to off Mansfield. "Ski-Ball and his brother Low-Low had been offered $25,000 each to take care of old Mansfield," Bunky said over and over in my head.

* * * *

"So, how rich are we, Cuz?"
"Bunky, do you know how we can reach Ski-Ball and Low-Low?"
"They were let out of the county about a week ago. I can find them."
"Can we go today?"
"Ain't nothing but a word, Cuz."
"I'll see you in a minute," I said, hanging up the phone.
The ghost still had some more talking to do.

Chapter 22
Ghosts in the Closet

I looked over at Bunky, always excited for an adventure. He probably would have made a good reporter if he hadn't done the drug dealing thing. He had a real knack, a real way of putting people at ease. He had sources, was always in the know, and he was leading me to Ski-Ball and Low-Low. I was hoping they would be able to shed some light on the second will, Red Mansfield's death, and the woman who propositioned them.

It wasn't difficult finding the brothers. They were directing traffic on Leonard Avenue, weaving in and out of traffic to stopped vehicles. They looked like a pair of wannabee rappers—white Ts, hats to the side, pants hanging to the ground, boxers showing prominently, and two pairs of Timberland boots. Just like twins, they did everything together—hustled together, been to jail together, and most likely would be heading back to jail together. In fact, where were the police?

"Hey, Ski-Ball and Low-Low, can I holla at you?" Bunky yelled out the window as we pulled our car over to the side. The brothers must have thought they had a major roller as they hustled over to my rented Cadillac, surprised to see Bunky in the driver's seat.

"My man, Bunky. Where'd you get the sweet ride? You must be living well, playa," Low-Low said, slapping Bunky's hand.

"Who you working with, Bunk man? Who is your connect? Put us on," Ski-Ball said.

I wondered if Bunky would tell the truth. He seemed at times incapable of avoiding exaggeration. I'm sure he was soaking up the admiration and slight groveling, so I was a bit surprised by what I heard next.

"This isn't my vehicle. It's my Cousin James's ride. Do you remember?

I talked to you about him when we were in the county," Bunky said. "I'm out of the game. I'm here trying to help my cousin. I need the 4-1-1."

Yeah, Bunky swore he didn't mention my name up while he was in the clink. But, considering the way he likes to talk.

I was surprised, however, that he was getting out of the business. If Aunt Dee had heard him say that, we would not have been able to get her off her knees thanking Jesus for this miracle.

"What type of information you need, Bunk? You interfering with our business now?" Ski-Ball said.

"I'm not going to keep you long. What can you tell me about the lady who approached you?"

"What lady? We got a whole lot of ladies approaching us. Don't we Low-Low?" Ski-Ball asked, turning to his twin.

"Sho you right, brother."

"I want to know about the woman you were talking up in the county. The one that wanted you to handle some Red business."

"We don't know what you're talking about. Ain't no one approach us about some Red business or any other business," Ski-Ball said.

"Oh, you going to play games with me now, Ski-Ball? Now, you can't talk to me after you and your brother talked my fucking ear off in the county?"

"Look Bunky. I don't know what you're talking about and I don't know the motherfucker sitting in your car. As far as I'm concerned, you could be sitting next to the feds."

"Come on y'all. I might not be slinging any longer, but that doesn't mean I'm turning narc. Like I said, this is my cousin. I only need some help locating this woman."

"I told you we ain't talk to no woman about anything. You have to bounce, Bunky. We have work to do. We ain't retired. Let's go Low-Low," Ski-Ball said as he walked toward a car parked across the street.

"Low-Low, you can't talk for yourself now? What, you ain't got nothin' to say now?" Bunky taunted.

Low-Low shook his head and started toward the car his brother already was leaning against, but suddenly turned around.

"We was talkin' shit, Bunky. You know how I like to run my mouth.

151

I was just repeating somethin' I heard. It was Tokey who told the story first."

With that Low-Low ran to his brother, who glared at him.

"Who is Tokey?" I asked.

"One of those bad niggas like Bigger Thomas that we read about in school," Bunky said chuckling. Yeah, Bunky had a little more depth than I had given to him. What did he know about *Native Son*? A lot more than I had given him credit for, apparently.

"How well do you know this Tokey," I asked.

"I know him well. This nigga is a killer fo sho. I don't believe some white woman approached his thuggish ass for anything. Ain't no man, and it don't matter what his color, gonna fuck with this nigga! In fact, I'm cussing myself out now for even considering trying to find this muthafucker... and he likes me."

"Don't tell me you're scared of a Tokey?" I said, cracking myself up.

"I didn't say I was scared of anyone. Don't get it twisted, Cuz. I just know who to fuck with and who not to fuck with. And Tokey is a dude you don't fuck with. I'm thinking those damn twins were lying. But we got to check out our sources—right, Cuz?"

"Yeah, we have to check out our sources," I said, smiling, as I pushed on with my cub reporter. Bunky pulled my Caddy up to a bar, a little hole in the wall. Including the bartender, there were only six people in the entire joint. A woman in her early forties walked with a shuffle as if she were pulling her leg along. She had dark shiny skin, plump, but not pleasantly. Two patrons sat at opposite ends of the bar—one guy looked barely sixteen (too young to be here) and the other had to be in his sixties. Their focal point, other than their beers, was the TV set, Judge Judy holding court.

"Ya know Judge Judy gonna side with dat white woman," the young man said.

"Judge Judy gonna side with any woman if a man is behind on child support," the older man countered. "Believe me, I know. I got five children and three baby mamas."

"I know dat. I gots two baby mamas myself," said the kid. "But dat nigga gonna take her car an he ain't gonna pay no child support? Dat's his ass."

"You probably right, young blood," the older guy said, taking a sip from his beer.

Standing near the pool table was truly a menacing man. He grimaced the entire time. He had the high balls and knocked one in the far right corner pocket. And with little joy, he knocked another ball in a side pocket. He knocked a third ball in the other side pocket. Each ball hit appeared to be in pain. He was pretty good. And with ease, he knocked the eight ball in the far left-hand corner pocket. His expression hadn't changed a bit. He still looked angry, even after his opponent grudgingly handed him a fifty-dollar bill.

"Hey, Toke, can I holla at you for a minute?" Bunky asked.

"Bunky, my man. What in the hell do you want? I'm trying to make money. I don't have time for any of your bullshit."

"No, bullshit, no hustle. Let me buy you a drink, Toke. What are you having?"

"I'll take a Johnny Walker Red if I have to listen to your bullshit."

"New Yoke, get a Johnny Walker Red for my man, get a rum and coke for me, and get yourself something," Bunky said, giving drink orders absent of money.

When I returned, it appeared that the two were pretty well engaged. Bunky was good. Tokey was no longer grimacing. In fact, it appeared he had a slight smile on his face as Bunky cracked jokes. On seeing me, Bunky grabbed the drinks, handed one to Tokey, and shooed me away. I went back to the bar, in drink and in thought, wondering where this was going. It looked like Bunky would get out of here with his head. In fact, the two appeared to be having a good time. Yeah, Bunky had a way with people. He was pretty smooth. I was finding myself liking and respecting him more and more the longer I stayed in Clayhatchee.

"Two more drinks, New Yoke," Bunky yelled out, not looking at me.

I should have been pissed, but I was more amused than anything else. Between running drinks for Tokey and Bunky, it gave me some time to reflect. I was thinking about ghosts. Red wasn't the only one. A lot of people around here—including the living—had been rattling chains around the family for years and no one heard. I thought I knew everything about my family. I didn't know a damn thing. I for damn sure didn't appreciate family, until now. Aunt Dee opened her home and heart to me. Bunky went to jail for me. Before this trip, we hadn't really known each other, but that common blood was enough for them to allow me into their world. They had been better at family than I had ever been to anyone. My brother and sisters had not penetrated my world. As far as I was concerned, they had their lives and I had mine. I'm not sure when I took that position, why I drifted off to an island all my own. It was just me and my pen, me and my thoughts— even Jackie couldn't reach me there. I can't blame her. But now it was different. I was ready to tear down that wall, to make it right with her, with my family. It was time for some changes.

"Time to go, Cuz," Bunky said, slapping hands with Tokey. "Hey, Toke, I'll be around your place next week. I got some new music I want you to hear."

"Solid, see you in a minute. Tell Cuz thanks for the drinks," Tokey said to Bunky, although I was standing next to Bunky.

"Cuz says you're welcome," Bunky offered, although I hadn't said anything, and was still standing next to him. Then Bunky surprised me. He grabbed me to head for the door and didn't say a word as he dragged me to my vehicle. The grabbing and silence startled me.

"What's your rush? You think Tokey is going to remember that he owes you an ass-whopping? I must say he is an intimidating fellow," I said, chuckling.

"I've known that nigga all my life. He's my boy. We had a rap group back in the day. We go way back."

"You acted like you didn't want to talk to him."

"I acted like I didn't want to fuck with him. He's not to be played with. But that's not what I want to talk about. I need to let you know what that nigga said."

Chapter 23
Handle That

Bunky was speaking so fast that I had to tell him to slow down. He didn't get this excited when we found the ghost dead. Bunky was nearly jumping out of his chest when he said.

"Tokey saw Red before he died," Bunky exclaimed. "But he didn't merk the ghost. Told me he was approached by his lawyer for some help in getting an old man to sign a document."

Now, my mind was racing.

"Tokey thought it was going to be easy money," Bunky continued. "Best of all, it gave him a chance to fuck with Red, who had scared the shit out us when we were kids. Tokey said that old goat didn't scare, he wouldn't sign the document. Toke roughed him up a little but not too much because he wasn't trying to have another body pinned on him. He said Red was breathing when he left."

"Are you buying his story?" I asked.

"He ain't got no reason to lie. Plus, he's still pissed that he wasn't paid for his troubles. His lawyer all but told him to kiss her ass when he asked for his money. And you know that didn't sit well with my man, who normally would have just knocked a disrespectful muthafucker out, man or woman. I guess she threatened him with all types of shit, like making sure he went back to prison if he asked about any money or if he didn't keep his mouth shut. Tokey's feelings were hurt."

"Why didn't he speak about this earlier when you were sitting in jail for Red's murder? Where was your boy then? Why is he talking now?"

"Look, for niggas out here, like everywhere else, it's self-preservation. I ain't mad at him. And the reason he's not worried about talking now is because he wants to make sure his name doesn't become implicated in this shit. It's all about self-preservation, Cuz. He thinks his lawyer might have had something to do with killing Red. She was more than pissed that he didn't get that signature, and she said she would have to take care of it herself."

"Who is his attorney?"

"Some bitch name Stealthfing, Stealhfick."

"Stealthman? Ann Stealthman?"

"Yeah, I think that's it. Yeah, that's what Tokey said. Ann Stealthman," Bunky said, pleased with himself.

"Interesting turn of events," I said, more to myself than to Bunky.

"What do you mean, Cuz?"

"It was Stealthman who came between us and our money. She introduced a document at the reading that said her client was the only beneficiary to Red's fortune. I knew Reverend Roy was shady but didn't think he was greedy enough to kill someone."

"You must be out of your mind," Bunky interrupted. "I know the good reverend you're talking about, man. Don't speak ill of the anointed. That man is damn near a saint around here. He's been tryin' to integrate long before it was fashionable. And now he has the biggest church in the South, Black or white. And you think the King of the Gospel is a murderer?"

"He's killed before."

"Reverend Roy?"

"The good reverend and his brother, most likely with the guidance and approval of Red Mansfield, killed Charles Jackson Jr. Red didn't like the budding romance between Charles and his daughter, my sister."

Bunky didn't say a word. He took out a near-empty pack of Newports and surgically went through his cigarette routine. Taking a long deep drag, he appeared lost in thought. After a minute, he put out the partially smoked cigarette, using the bottom of his left Timberland boot.

"What are we going to do now, James?"

"I'm thinking, Cuz."

CARLISLE

"We have blood on our hands, Red, and you must repent, as I did. We both know it is all part of God's plan that our paths crossed. If I had not gone to prison, I would not have been saved by His grace. If you had never paid me $30,000 to keep my mouth shut about Charles Jackson, I could not have built my church and spread the gospel to a beautiful group of people. Now, you must sacrifice again, my friend. God wants you to make this right, to seek salvation. Sign the will, Red."

Reverend Roy stared at the old man standing on his tiptoes, trying to keep his balance.

"You have no other choice but to sign this will," the reverend continued, his demeanor suddenly turning to rage. "Sign the damn paper you decrepit son of a bitch. Make amends for your past. Seek salvation through me. I will kill you, Red. You know I will."

At that moment, Red began to chuckle. How utterly bizarre that he would die at the hands of these two men—the reverend in front and the child behind. Red laughed and laughed until he could not laugh anymore. He just fluttered, danced, and dangled to the horror of his two killers, who could do nothing more than cry out as the ghost floated away.

Chapter 24
Two White Crackers

The first thing I noticed when I returned to Mansfield's street was a rickety old house at the bottom of the hill. It appeared unlivable, although two white, teenage boys were sitting on the front steps. I stopped the car but kept it running for the air conditioning. The weather was so hot and humid even the boys in their shorts and tank tops looked overdressed. On top of the hill sat Mansfield's mansion; injured, bruised, and bandaged with yellow tape crisscrossed on the front door warning humans not to trespass. As I fumbled to retrieve my notebook from the backseat, someone was knocking on my window.

"You 5-0?" asked a young white boy with blonde hair. He couldn't have been more than sixteen.

"Naw."

"You need something?"

"I'm not trying to score drugs if that's what you're peddling."

The boy leaned forward into my car and I noticed his soft features.

"I'm not pushing drugs, baby. You look like you want company. I don't get too many Johns riding on this street with such nice cars. You either a baller or a preacher driving a car this fancy. I'm good with both, no judgment."

"You get many preachers around these parts?"

"Just one. So, you want company or what?"

"I'll pay you for your time. But let's just talk."

"Whatever you want big baller; you're paying."

"I'd like to know about your preacher."

"Gonna cost more if you want me to tell you about my Roy Toy," he teased. "My name's Jody."

Jody told me he and his friends found the deserted, out-of-the-way street in front of Mansfield's home a perfect hookup spot. To my pleasant surprise, Jody was loquacious. He was nineteen, although he had been tricking since he was fifteen.

"I came out in high school," he said. "My parents are old-school Christians, so they suggested that conversion therapy would solve my particular ailment. They said unless I would let Jesus deliver me, I could take my homosexual spirit and vacate their home."

Jody told me he was good with leaving because he was more than ready to deliver himself from his parents, Jesus, and the church. He found salvation on the streets and was delivered by his wits and ass. I'm guessing it was the last item that attracted Reverend Roy to him. No matter your tastes, the boy was pretty.

"Yeah, Reverend Roy used to spend a lot of time on this block, visiting the old man up on the hill," Jody said. "The reverend was kind, tender, and paid handsomely. He would always tell me his only interest was to bring me back to my Christian roots. Roy Toy had a passion for the Bible and anal. He even offered to shelter me at his church. I didn't need to be that close to Jesus, again, so I declined. But that was no problem because we would go directly to his house."

"Do you still see him?" I asked.

"Hah, hardly," he grumbled. "Told me a couple of months ago that his longtime boyfriend would be visiting, and we would have to put our relationship on pause. Tell you the truth, what hurt me the most was losing the steady coin. But then I saw the boyfriend, and he was a frickin' old man. Not as old as Roy Toy, but at least in his fifties."

"When did you see him?"

"The two of them were hustling out of the old man's house up there as if the Devil himself was on their tails. Roy Toy was so focused on getting into his giant car and blastin' down this street, he never even looked my way. I was right there on the porch. It was almost comical, both of them looked scared silly."

Chapter 25
Secret Places

We pulled up to Reverend Roy's driveway, and it was as opulent as I thought it would be. He had a gate that stretched across the driveway and attached itself to marble pillars. On top of the pillars sat the head of gold-colored lions. The house looked to be three stories and layered like a wedding cake. The house had a shine to it—hard to look at it directly. A voice came on the intercom.

"How may I help you?"

"Hi, this is James Kingsman and Bunky, I mean Walter Macklin. We would like to see Reverend Roy."

"Certainly, I will see if he's available," said the voice.

Bunky and I looked at each other, knowing we were about to be shut down. Surprisingly, the gate swung open.

We were led into the house by an elderly Black man wearing a white coat and gloves. He was a skinny man in his eighties with a half-moon baldness that was punctuated with silver hair along the sides.

"This way, gentlemen," the servant said, leading us through more opulence. His place brimmed with gold. I couldn't tell if we were in the home of a reverend or a rapper. We were led into his office, where we found the reverend plopped behind his mammoth oak desk. The bling didn't stop with his house. The reverend wore two gold pinky rings around his fat pinkies and he draped his neck with a huge gold chain. His wrist was adorned with a gold Rolex. Yeah, Rev. Roy was big time. He took his time before acknowledging our presence, a deliberate pause.

"Please have a seat. I'm sure you men have pressing business, so let's get to it," the reverend said, smiling but not really. "You are here to discuss the will. The judge will be making his decision tomorrow, is that correct?"

"Yes," I said, "but I want to talk about Red Mansfield's death."

The reverend shifted in his seat, seeming irritated with me already. He leaned and slouched in his seat and his smile became wider or wilder. I couldn't really tell.

"Aren't you done asking questions about Red Mansfield?"

"Did you kill Mansfield?"

"Now, why would I want to hang an old man? If he hadn't been killed, he would have been dead in a year, two years… three years tops. There really was no need for anyone to rush the natural process, to hurry God's time."

"I could think of a million little reasons," Bunky inserted.

"I'm rich beyond my wildest dreams. I've been blessed. I don't need Red's money. I got God's money. I have God's favor. He delivered me from being the son of a dirt farmer with no education to becoming the head of a congregation with thousands of believers. I don't need Red's money at all. You boys should come to Sunday's service… we don't discriminate against drug dealers nor Yankees."

"No thank you," I said. "Let's talk about the money. The will no one knew about states that you will receive all of Red Mansfield's money. How did you swing that? Why was Red so generous with you?"

Again, Reverend Roy shifted in his chair and smiled, but not really a smile.

"That's the question I should be asking you. When and how did your family become so familiar with Red Mansfield that he was planning to leave you ten percent of his estate? As far as I know, Red went to his grave the way he lived, hating Black folks."

"I guess God works in mysterious ways, Reverend," I said.

"Indeed, He does. And the Lord knows money coming to me rather than your family would be put to better use. I did some investigation of my own and found some disturbing things about your family— convicts, single mothers, drug addicts. None of them are worthy of this much money, not even a fancy reporter like yourself."

"This is what I think, Reverend. Before you killed Red, you had him sign a false will that left you and your church with everything. Is that how it went down?"

"You Yankees have wild imaginations. Y'all still think the war was about slavery and you were the victors," said Rev. Roy, punctuated with a guffaw.

"Well, Reverend Roy Toy, maybe you'll trust the imagination of your gay rebel friend, Jody. He saw you running out of Red's house the evening of the hanging. It wouldn't take much to get Jody to tell the police. I'm not trying to get you jammed up. I just want answers."

The reverend shifted his girth again in his leather office chair. He leaned forward and looked directly at me with an intent and seriousness I had not seen before from the good reverend.

"If I had killed Red," Roy growled, "it wouldn't be for money. Red Mansfield took a great deal from my family. He owed me."

"What do you mean he owes you?"

"He owes me the life of my brother. He left us to take the fall and my brother never recovered. Hell, I barely recovered. If it hadn't been for Jesus, I would have killed myself, just like Jack. After we got out of prison, my brother couldn't find peace anywhere but the bottle. At some point, the bottle wasn't enough. I tried to bring him to Jesus, but poor Jack, rest his soul, was too far gone."

"What does that have to do with Red?"

"It has everything to do with Red," Rev. Roy furiously barked, slamming his fat fingers into the chess set on his desk, sending marble rooks, knights, kings, queens, and pawns airborne. Funny, the bishops, although on their sides, stayed on the board.

Red took several breaths to regain his composure, but he was incensed.

"That bastard asked us to do a favor for him when we were young, just boys, and he left us holding the bag. He got away from it scot-free."

"Are you talking about the Jackson boy's death?"

"That's all I've been talking about, son. Red wanted that boy dead and when we killed him, Red washed his hands of us. We were disconnected from him. He despised us and, worse than that, acted as if we didn't exist. We existed all right. We took his time in a crappy prison and we lost everything. Our mama died because of Red. That lying son of a bitch went to his grave saying that he only wanted us

CARLISLE

to scare the Jackson boy, but that's not the truth. Red wanted blood. He might not have said the words, but he wanted blood, and when we gave him blood, he turned on us."

"So, killing Red was for revenge?"

"No, no, no. Have you not understood anything that I've said? Vengeance is in the hands of the Lord. Killing Red was a reckoning. Red was the blood sacrifice if we were ever going to move from the old South to the new South. Red was a relic from the past. Every time he came out of his haunted mansion, he was a reminder of the old time where the coloreds were not allowed to drink from the same water fountains, go to same schools as whites, eat at any diner, sit where they wanted to on the bus. He was a reminder of our hateful past. I am building something bigger. I'm bringing the races together. I need all his money. He had to go. Killing Red was doing God's work. It was God's will."

I turned around to Bunky, who was shaking his head and chuckling.

"Bunky, did you get all of this?"

"I got it all recorded," Bunky said, lifting the mini-tape recorder in the air for Rev. Roy to see.

"Thank you for the confession, Reverend," I said.

"That was not a confession," he yelled, quickly turning and extending a hand toward Bunky. "Son, you don't know what you're doing. Just give me the recorder."

"Ain't gonna be able to do that," Bunky said. "Some of those white boys at the police station don't go for all that race mixing you've been preaching. They are gonna be happy as hell to hear you confessing. This might even get me in good with them lawmen crackers."

As Bunky laughed, a small man suddenly burst through a door stationed directly behind Rev. Roy's desk. He stopped at the reverend's side, grabbing his hand and ignoring us.

"Why are you telling these people all these lies?"

"Go back to the study," Rev. Roy said, not even looking at the man. This must be the partner, a perfect fit to Jody's description— short blonde hair, clean shaven, late middle age. And he was fit, that's for sure. He wore a gray form-fitting T-shirt, white jeans, and some sandals. He seemed out of place. Really out of place.

And there was another study?

"I will not go back to the study," the man protested. "And you did not kill anybody. Tell them the truth, Roy."

"Robert, I'm not going to tell you again!"

Robert?

"The reverend didn't do anything wrong. I know… "

"Stop, Robert!"

"The reverend wouldn't hurt anyone. He's been the only good thing in this community for years. He's spreading the gospel and God's love. He's bringing the races together. You can't take that recorder to the police. You can't destroy this man and all he's done."

Reverend Roy stood up from his desk.

"Robert E., I'm asking you to leave now. I'll take care of this."

Robert E? Is this Red's son? What in the world? With Roy Willowbrook?

The reverend had wrapped his arms around Robert, who was crying like a child. Strange, Reverend Roy exhibited a tenderness I didn't know he had. Gone was the flash, the façade, the self-righteousness.

"Shall I call the Scotland Yard or you?" Bunky asked me in his best British accent.

"I'll call," I said, pulling my phone out.

"Put the phone down," ordered the reverend, breaking his hug with Robert and stepping away from his desk.

Just as quickly, Robert E. opened the top desk drawer, pulling out a pistol.

"You have to hear me out," said Robert E., pointing the pistol in our direction. Both Bunky and I took a step back, frozen.

"Okay, we're listening. You can lower the gun. Are you Robert E. Mansfield?"

"This man you are trying to put in prison is a good man," sobbed Robert, ignoring my question. "Don't you understand this?"

Bunky and I both nodded.

"He's a good man. I love this man. He accepted me when my own daddy wouldn't. I can't let you take this man to jail for a lie. He didn't kill my daddy. I did."

CARLISLE

Rev. Roy slumped back to his desk chair, holding his head with both hands as he leaned forward, propped up only by his elbows. I saw one more look from this man that hadn't been present until now—defeat.

"Why would you kill your own pappy?" Bunky asked.

"He was never a father to me," said Robert, seemingly regaining some of his composure. "When he found out that I liked men, I was probably lower than any Black person in Clayhatchee. He couldn't stomach having a queer as a son, and he treated me as if I didn't exist. Besides, he had Katherine. She was the one he loved. He had Katherine."

"What happened?" I asked. "Why would you kill him?"

"I didn't mean to kill him. Lord knows. I just went with Reverend Roy to scare Daddy into signing the new will. Daddy needed to sign. The money is going for a wonderful cause. It's going to help with our racial reconciliation ministry. We are going to bring more people to Christ with our message of love. That's what we're all about here. Love. Black. White. Straight. Gay. We love everyone. I didn't want to hurt Daddy. We were just talking to him. We just wanted to scare him. But then he started laughing, and he wouldn't stop. He was laughing hysterically, mocking me like he used to do when I was a little boy. I tried to stop him, and I accidentally knocked over the chair. I tried to get him back on the chair. We both did. It was an accident."

"Okay, Robert E.," said Rev. Roy. "They know it was accident. Hand me the gun now."

"They have to believe it was an accident. They have to believe you had nothing to do with Father's death."

"We believe. We believe," Bunky said, nodding his head forcefully.

"We believe you, Robert E., just put down the gun," I said, hoping Robert E. was more stable than he looked and sounded.

"Do you still have that tape recorder?"

"Yeah, I have it," Bunky said holding it up. "Do you want it?"

"No. I want you to press record."

And Bunky did just that, Robert E. recounting his entire story.

"Did you get it all?"

Bunky nodded yes.

"Take that to the police. The church doesn't need to suffer. Roy doesn't need to suffer. Roy, you know I love you. Do you know that?" Rev. Roy nodded his head and spoke with his eyes.

"Roy, I'm sorry, my love... " and with that, Robert E. Mansfield put the gun to his chest and pulled the trigger.

Bunky dropped to the floor, and then had the good sense of grabbing the gun now abandoned. I had been too stunned and paralyzed to move. And then there was Roy, holding Robert E. in his arms, caressing his hair in a fit of tears. This was the clearest I had seen the reverend... stripped of his robe.

The police did not take long to get to Rev. Roy's house. By the time they arrived, Reverend Roy was coming to his senses, his public self. He didn't say a word until the first officer walked in with his gun drawn.

"They murdered my congregant. Arrests these men!"

Bunky was ordered to put the gun down as two officers trained their weapons on us. Bunky carefully complied. He was handcuffed. I was handcuffed. As we were being read our rights, to our protestations, Reverend Roy was being examined by paramedics.

"Officer, would you check the pockets of one of those boys? I believe one of them is trying to leave with my recorder," Rev. Roy said.

The short officer, who looked to be in his early forties, searched my pockets and then Bunky's, fishing out the recorder.

"Is this your recorder, Reverend?" the officer said, holding it in the air with his right hand.

"It is indeed. Thank you so much," Rev. Roy said as he reached for the device.

"He's lying," I yelled. "That recorder is evidence. Please don't give it to him. Play the recorder."

"That's nonsense officer," Roy calmly responded. "That recorder is mine, and it's just one of several items these hoodlums had planned to steal from my home. I would be lying here dead if my servants hadn't called the police, if you all hadn't shown up."

"Whose is this? I don't want any games," one of the officers said, taking a closer look at the recorder. "This says, *Property of the New York Daily News*."

Reverend Roy lunged, trying to grab the recorder, but had his hand smacked by a police baton, sending the meaty preacher into the wall, where he sat slumped.

"Sorry Reverend, this is evidence," said the officer.

After reading Reverend Roy his rights, the police had to drag him to the squad car. Roy was shouting with the fervor of a Sunday morning sermon, promising fire and brimstone to rain down on those officers, on us, and on his beloved southern community that would miss him. His rant included prophesy of a most certain race riot to occur. He was the only savior in this community. That he alone could stop this race Armageddon.

I was finally done here in the South, except for one thing—I had a story to write.

Chapter 26
Unearthing

Reverend Roy's arrest became national news, picked up by all the major networks. Of course, I broke the story, and it felt good. I think I even got a smile from my editor.

"You didn't screw up this story," Cuddy said when he called. "When will you be back? Vacation is over, Kingsman. I better see your ass in your seat Monday morning. Got to go. Some of us still have to work for a living."

Oh, I couldn't wait to get back to work. I couldn't wait to get back to New York. This trip had drained me. Probably nothing was more emotional than talking to Mildred about her brother's confession and death. It seemed all too much for her. She hadn't seen Robert E. since she was sixteen. One day he just walked out of the house and never returned. Her mother and father never mentioned him, at least not in front of her. Mildred had heard rumors about her brother and the Willowbrook boy, but those were just rumors. All she knew for certain was that Robert E. had vanished, she was not to speak of him, and she had to grieve in silence for the young man she remembered as sensitive and loving and protective of her.

"Once I became an adult, I searched for him more than once, but each time coming to a dead-end," she said to me. "As the years passed, I thought he was most likely dead. And now, his story is all over the news. James, you know more about Robert E. in the last forty years than anyone."

Not exactly. I had gotten my information by visiting Reverend Roy in jail. He was shaken and angry, but spoke willingly about Robert E. He wanted to clear his love's good name.

* * * *

"He was a teenager when he ran away from Clayhatchee," said the reverend. "Robert E. moved to Boston, where he alternated from going to school and working a series of odd jobs."

"I understand he was a professor," I said.

"No, in fact, he never finished college. Instead, he became a devoted activist to the anti-war and civil rights movements. And as he became more enmeshed in the movement for racial equality, he grew spiritually as a person. He became a faithful member of a non-denominational, diverse church in Boston."

"How did you meet?"

"I was the young Reverend Roy Willowbrook from a place I expected no one in Boston had ever heard of... Clayhatchee, Alabama. At that time, I was still doing prison ministry and was invited to conduct a series of messages on racial reconciliation. Robert was doing volunteer work in prison ministry and had seen I was from his hometown. We hit it off immediately, discussing racial integration, helping imprisoned people find the gospel, and making a positive change in the South."

"Small world," I said.

"Indeed, we fell in love and vowed to make a life together fighting hate. We had no idea of our connection to Red Mansfield. Robert E. had changed his last name, choosing to use his mother's maiden name. He vaguely remembered the story surrounding the Jackson boy and my name did not register. But we were both floored when we figured it out."

At first, they planned to return to Clayhatchee to take their message of racial reconciliation to the belly of the beast, as Roy proclaimed. It was Robert's idea to solicit Red for seed money to build their megachurch. But he also understood that Roy's chances of achieving success would only come if he remained hidden. For years, they met secretly in New England, sometimes halfway in Virginia. To everyone else, Robert E. Mansfield had completely vanished, his clandestine life with Reverend Roy a well-planned secret.

* * * *

"He was alive the entire time and I didn't know," said Mildred. "And now, it's too late."

The brother she thought was dead had been resurrected just to die again. So strange that they both had deserted their old lives to become their real selves—Mildred as a Black woman and Robert E. as a gay man.

"We never had a chance to share our lives," Mildred said, shaking her head.

"I know, Mildred," I said, giving her a hug. "But you still have two little brothers and two younger sisters. You're not alone. You have a family that loves you. I love you, Sis."

"Thank you, James. I love you too."

Chapter 27
Dear Mama

The trip home wouldn't be as solitary as the one I took getting there. I asked Mildred to take the drive back with me and to my surprise and happiness, she said yes. The nineteen-hour journey would give us time to get to know each other. She was planning to stay with me for a couple of months; during that time, I would have my brother and sisters to my home as well. They were eager to bond with Mildred. We also needed to iron out our new good money fortunes. The Kingsman family had money. Who knew? I was looking forward to family time. Mama knew exactly what she was doing. Maybe this was her plan all along.

I caught myself smiling, but I didn't know why—for Mama, my family, Mildred, Jackie? I told Jackie I was ready, more than ready, to be a family man, and she was ready to take another chance on me. She told me she had always been ready to be my wife. She was waiting on me. Now, she saw something new in me, a man invested in others, a man who realized worth in familial ties.

Jackie and I started looking for dates. We thought about a June wedding at home—not in New York, not in Pittsburgh, but Clayhatchee, Alabama. I wanted to spend more time with my southern family in my ancestral home. Jackie and Mildred were on board, Aunt Dee was ecstatic, and Bunky was planning my bachelor party with the promise of a room full of "hoochie mamas."

In October, I flew back to Clayhatchee for Roy Willowbrook's trial. Taking the advice of his new attorney, the reverend plead guilty to escape the death penalty. The prosecution did not see Red's death as innocent or accidental; not with the planning, threatening, extorting, and lifting old

Red up on that chair. Reverend Roy was sentenced to life in prison without the possibility of parole.

Did I mention Ann Stealthman? After being disbarred, the sleazy attorney was sentenced to ten years in prison. Most of the folks in Clayhatchee thought she got off easy. Not so with the other verdict. As unseemly as Reverend Roy's deeds had been with Red's death and the revelation of his love affair in the conservative red belt community, the preacher still had his share of supporters who thought his life sentence too harsh.

"I think they should have fried his ass," Bunky said, laughing.

"Bunky, watch yo mouth," Aunt Dee admonished. "I'll take a switch to you."

"It's true, Mama. You know that."

"What I know is God's grace. We all need God's grace, even Reverend Roy. A lot of Black folks love dat man, so dere must be some good in him."

"Aunt Dee, you sound like my mama," I said.

"I guess I do, James. I guess I do."

THE END

About the Author

Anthony Todd Carlisle, Ph.D., is married to Amy Alexander, Ph.D., and has two children, Arielle and Amya. He is an associate professor in the Department of Culture, Media, and Performance at California University of Pennsylvania.

Carlisle was a reporter for 11 years. He worked for the *New Pittsburgh Courier*, *Daily News*, *Pittsburgh Business Times*, *Beaver County Times* and *Pittsburgh Tribune-Review*. During those years, he worked in several beat areas: city government, urban affairs, religion, education, transportation, labor and sports as a business. As a reporter, he won several awards, including Robert L. Vann Award for feature writing and investigative reporting and the Keystone State Spotlight Award for first place business story.

Carlisle is also a veteran, having served in the United States Army Reserve for 14 years, reaching the rank of captain. He worked as both a supply officer and a military journalist. In 2003, he was deployed to the Middle East as part of Operation Iraqi Freedom. Upon his return, he was awarded California University of Pennsylvania's Presidential Medal for Patriotic Service.